***That voice sounded so familiar.
Impossibly familiar.***

Unable to stop herself, Lucy began to turn around, wondering if her ears—and all her other senses—were deceiving her. After all, six years was a long time. What were the odds that she'd bump into him here?

Ross Marshall.

"Oh, my God," he whispered, shocked, frozen, staring as thoroughly as she was. "Lucy?"

She nodded slowly, not taking her eyes off him, wondering why the years had made him even more attractive.

The man was gorgeous. Truly, without-a-doubt, mouth-wateringly handsome, every bit as hot as the first time she'd laid eyes on him.

He'd been her first lover. They'd shared an amazing holiday season. But after that one Christmas, they had never seen each other again.

Until now.

Dear Reader,

I'm a big kid when it comes to Christmas. I love the music and the decorations and the wrapping...the whole holiday feeling in the air.

But many years ago, I realized how difficult Christmas can be when it's associated too closely with a loss. Christmas of 1989 was incredibly painful for me. Only because I had a one-year-old baby and a wonderful husband was I able to dig myself out of my sadness and try to enjoy the holidays, for their sake.

Remembering those feelings, and drawing on that, I started thinking about a story...about a woman who tries to avoid any kind of "traditional" Christmas because it's just too hard for her to celebrate a holiday when she has lost the parents who made it so very special for her throughout her life. I loved creating Lucy, the heroine of *It Happened One Christmas*, who learns to find joy and happiness in the season again, because of a very special man.

I hope you enjoy Lucy and Ross's story and that you feel just a hint of that Christmas magic in the pages that follow.

Merry Christmas to all!

Leslie Kelly

AMSTERDAM PARIS SYDNEY HAMBURG
STOCKHOLM ATHENS TOKYO MILAN MADRID
PRAGUE WARSAW BUDAPEST AUCKLAND

Leslie Kelly

IT HAPPENED ONE CHRISTMAS

TORONTO NEW YORK LONDON
AMSTERDAM PARIS SYDNEY HAMBURG
STOCKHOLM ATHENS TOKYO MILAN MADRID
PRAGUE WARSAW BUDAPEST AUCKLAND

Recycling programs
for this product may
not exist in your area.

ISBN-13: 978-0-373-79658-8

IT HAPPENED ONE CHRISTMAS

ABOUT THE AUTHOR

Leslie Kelly has written dozens of novels for the Harlequin Blaze, Temptation and HQN lines. Known for her sparkling dialogue and humor, Leslie has been honored with numerous awards, including a National Readers' Choice Award. In 2010, she received the Lifetime Achievement Award in Series Romance from *RT Book Reviews*. Leslie lives in Maryland with her husband and their three daughters. Visit her online at www.lesliekelly.com.

Books by Leslie Kelly

To get the inside scoop on Harlequin Blaze and its talented writers, be sure to check out blazeauthors.com.

Don't miss any of our special offers. Write to us at the following address for information on our newest releases.

Harlequin Reader Service
U.S.: 3010 Walden Ave., P.O. Box 1325, Buffalo, NY 14269
Canadian: P.O. Box 609, Fort Erie, Ont. L2A 5X3

This one's dedicated to the Blaze Babes.
It's such a pleasure being one of you.

Merry Christmas!

1

Now
Chicago, December 23, 2011

WHEN LUCY FLEMING HAD been asked to photograph a corporate Christmas event, she'd envisioned tipsy assistants perched on the knees of grabby executives. Too much eggnog, naked backsides hitting the glass-topped copier, somebody throwing up in a desk drawer, hanky-panky in the janitor's closet—in short, a typical high-end work party where people forgot they were professionals and played teenager-at-the-frat-party, building memories and reputations that would take an entire year to live down.

She'd been wrong. Completely wrong.

Elite Construction, who'd hired her a few days ago when their previous photographer had bailed on them, had chosen to go a different, and much more wholesome, route. They were hosting an afternoon event, a family party for all of their employees as well as important clients, and whoever they cared to bring along—including small children. Catered food, from caviar to corn dogs, appealed to every palate. There were presents beneath a huge tree, pretty decorations, music filled with jingling bells and lots of smiles. It was almost enough to give a non-Christmas person like herself a little holiday tingle.

Oh. Except for the fact that she was working with a *very* cranky Kris Kringle.

"If they think I'm staying late, they can bite me. I got paid for three hours, not a minute more."

"We're almost done," she told the costumed man, whose bowl-full-of-jelly middle appeared homemade.

If only his nature were as true-to-character as his appearance. Though, she had to admit, right at this particular moment, his foul mood was understandable. He'd had to go dry his pants under a hand-dryer in the men's room after one boy had gotten so excited he'd peed himself. And Santa.

To be fair, Santa wasn't the only fraud around here this afternoon. Her own costume didn't exactly suit her personality, either. She felt like an idiot in the old elf getup, a leftover from her college days. But the kids loved it. And a happy, relaxed kid made for an easy-to-shoot kid...and great pictures.

All in all, she'd have to say this event had been a great success. Both for Elite Construction—whose employees had to be among the happiest in the city today—and for herself. Since moving back to Chicago from New York ten months ago, she'd been trying to build her business up to the level of success she'd had back east. Things were getting better—much—but a quick infusion of cash for an easy afternoon's work definitely helped.

Finally, after the last child in line had been seen to,

Lucy eyed the chubby man in red. "I think that's about it." She glanced at a clock on the wall. "Five minutes to spare."

"Damn good thing," he said. "God, I hate kids."

Lucy's mouth fell open; she couldn't help gawking. "Then why on earth do you do this?"

He pointed toward himself—his white hair, full beard, big belly. "What else am I gonna do, play the Easter bunny?"

Not unless he wanted to terrify every child on earth into swearing off candy. "Bet you can land a part in the stage version of *The Nightmare Before Christmas*," she mumbled. He sure looked like the Oogie Boogie man. And was about as friendly.

Lucy turned to the children lingering around the edges of the area that had been set up as "Santa's Workshop"—complete with fluffy fake snow, a throne and stuffed reindeer. Whoever had decorated for this party had really done a fantastic job. These kids had already had their turn on the big guy's lap, but were still crowded around the crotchety St. Nick. "It's time for Santa to get back to his workshop so he can finish getting ready for his big sleigh ride tomorrow night," she announced. "Santa, do you want to say anything before you leave?"

Father Friggin' Christmas grimaced and brushed cookie crumbs off his lap as he rose. "Be good or you won't get nothin'," he told them, adding a belly laugh to try to take the sting out of the words. His feigned heartiness fooled everyone under the age of ten, but certainly none of the adults. Waddling through the crowd toward the elevator, he didn't stop to pat one youngster on the head, or tickle a single chin.

Jerk.

For her part, Lucy found the little ones in their party clothes and patent leather shoes irresistible. Sweet, happy, so filled with life and laughter and excitement. There was one boy who was so photogenic he ought to be on the cover of a magazine, and she was dying to talk to his parents about a formal sitting.

You've come a long way, baby.

A very long way. To think she'd once vowed to never take a Santa photo, equating kid portraiture with one of Dante's circles of hell.

When she'd first set her sites on photography for her future, she'd argued with her brother over leaving Chicago to go to NYU to study. Then they'd argued when she'd decided to go from there to Europe, insisting she didn't want to take baby's-first-haircut pictures, dreaming instead of high fashion. Models and travel and exotic locations and *French Vogue* magazine covers.

She'd done all of that. Well, except for the magazine cover, though one of her shots had landed in a fashion week edition.

Yet, when all was said and done, she'd ended up finding her niche, her innermost talent and her satisfaction, back in the good old U.S. of A., working with children. It was, in this business, her claim to fame. Frankly, she was damn good at it. She'd made a name for herself in New York, her signature being the use of one color image in black and white shots. A toy, a piece of candy, a shirt or bandanna…something bright and sassy that demanded attention. Just like her photographs did.

Now she needed to drum up the same level of business in Chicago—which, despite her having been gone for so many years, was still her hometown. No, she'd never imagined moving back here, but when her brother, Sam, had gone through a messy divorce and seemed so lonely, she'd decided family came before anything else. She was all he had, and vice versa. So she'd returned.

Talk about changing your plans. Who'd have imagined it? Certainly not Lucy. And not her best friend from college, Kate, who still laughed about both her change in career path and in residence. Kate remembered Lucy's home-and-kids-are-boring stance in the old days.

Kate. She needed to give the other woman a call. Lucy hadn't seen her friend since she'd moved, though she and Kate kept in touch with frequent calls. Kate's two children were the ones who'd really opened her mind to the wondrous possibilities of tiny faces and hands and smiles, and she wanted to make sure their Christmas presents had arrived in time.

Those gifts—and working this party in the ridiculous getup—were about the sum total of her Christmas activities this year. Her brother had to work the whole weekend, cops not getting every holiday off the way civilians did. And though she was now back near the Chicago suburb where she'd grown up, she no longer had any close friends here who might have invited her over.

Not that she would have gone. Lucy avoided Christmas like the plague, and had for years. She'd just as soon pretend the holiday wasn't happening.

Most people would probably think that pathetic; Lucy found it a relief. Especially since the weatherman was saying a storm to rival the one at the start of Rudolph the Red Nosed Reindeer was on the way. It was supposed to roll in tonight and shut down the city with a couple of feet of the white stuff by Christmas morning. Sounded like an excellent time to be locked in her warm apartment with her Kindle and a bunch of chocolate and wine. Or chocolate wine—her new addiction.

Eyeing the gray sky through the expansive wall of windows, she began to pack up her gear. The party was winding down, only a dozen or so people remaining on this floor, which had been transformed from cubicles and meeting rooms to a holiday funland. She smiled at those nearest to her, then, seeing the glances at her silly hat, reached up to tug it off her head.

Before she could do it, however, she heard a voice. A deep, male voice—smooth and sexy, and so not Santa's.

"I hear that you did a terrific job."

Lucy didn't respond, letting her brain process what she was hearing. Her whole body had stiffened, the hairs on the back of her neck standing up, her skin tightening into tiny goose bumps. Because that voice sounded familiar. *Impossibly* familiar.

It can't be.

"It sounds like the kids had a great time."

Unable to stop herself, she began to turn around, wondering if her ears—and all her other senses—were deceiving her. After all, six years was a long time, the mind could play tricks. What were the odds that she'd bump into *him* here? And today of all days. December 23. *Six years exactly.* Was that really possible?

One look—and the accompanying frantic thudding

of her heart—and she knew her ears and brain were working just fine. Because it was *him*. Ross Marshall.

"Oh, my God," he whispered, shocked, frozen, staring as intently as she was. "Lucy?"

She nodded slowly, not taking her eyes off him, wondering why the years had made him even more attractive than ever. It didn't seem fair, or just. Not when she'd spent the past six years thinking he must have started losing that thick, golden-brown hair, or added a spare tire to that trim, muscular form or lost some of the sparkle from those green eyes.

Huh-uh.

The man was gorgeous. Truly, without-a-doubt, mouthwateringly handsome, and every bit as hot as he'd been the first time she'd laid eyes on him. But he wasn't that young, lean, hungry-looking guy anymore. Now he was all fully realized, powerful, strong—and devastatingly attractive—man.

She'd been twenty-two when they met, he two years older. And during the brief time they'd spent together, Ross had blown away all her preconceived notions of who she was, what she wanted and what she would do when the right guy came along.

He'd been her first lover.

They'd shared an amazing holiday season. But after that one Christmas, they had never seen each other again. Until now.

Well, doesn't this just suck?

"Hello, Ross," she murmured, wondering when her life had become a comedy movie. Because wasn't this always the way those things opened? The plucky, un-lucky-in-love heroine coming face-to-face with the one guy she'd never been able to forget while dressed in a ridiculous costume? It was right out of central casting 101—what else could she be wearing other than a short green dress with bells and holly on the collar, red-and-white striped hose, pointy-toed shoes and the dippy green hat with the droopy feather? The only thing that could make the scene more perfect was if she'd been draped across the grouchy Santa's lap, trying to evade his gropey hands, when the handsome hero came up to rescue her.

He did rescue you once. Big time.

Her heart twisted, as it always did when she thought about that... The way Ross had been there for her in what could have been a horrible moment. Whatever had happened later—however much she resented him now—she would never forget that he'd been there to keep her from getting hurt.

But that had been a long time ago. She was no longer that girl and she no longer needed any man's rescue.

"It's really you," he murmured.

"In the flesh."

"I can't believe it."

"That makes two of us," she admitted.

Her brain scrambled to find more words, to form thoughts or sentences. But she just couldn't. If she'd woken up this morning to find her bed had floated up into the sky on a giant helium balloon, she couldn't have been more surprised than she was right now.

Or more disturbed.

Because she wasn't supposed to see him again. Wasn't supposed to care again. Wasn't supposed to even think of getting hurt by him again.

She'd played this scene once, and at exactly this time of year. No way was she ready for a repeat.

She knew all that, knew it down to her soul. So why, oh why, was her heart singing? Crazy expression that, but it was true. There was music in her head and brightness in her eyes and a smile fought to emerge on her lips.

Because it was Ross. The guy she'd met *exactly* six years ago today. The man she'd fallen crazy in love with.

At Christmastime.

2

Then
New York, December 23, 2005

Hmm. Decisions, decisions.

Lucy honestly wasn't sure what would be the best tool for the job. After all, it wasn't every day she was faced with a project of this magnitude. As a photography student at NYU, she usually spent more time worrying about creating things rather than hacking them up.

Big knife? No, she might not get the right angle and could end up cutting herself.

Scissors? Probably not strong enough to cut through *that*.

Razor? She doubted her Venus was up to the task, and had no idea how to get one of those old-fashioned straight-edged ones short of robbing a barber.

A chainsaw or a hatchet?

Probably overkill. And killing wasn't the objective.

After all, she didn't really want to kill Jude Zacharias. She just wanted to separate him from his favorite part of his cheating anatomy. AKA: the part he'd cheated with.

Lucy didn't even realize she'd been mumbling aloud. Not until her best friend, Kate, who sat across from her in this trendy Manhattan coffee-and-book shop interjected, "You're not going to cut off his dick, so stop fantasizing about it."

Nobody immediately gasped at Kate's words, so obviously they hadn't been overheard. Not surprising—they were tucked in a back corner of the café. Plus, Beans & Books was crowded with shoppers frenzied by the realization that they only had one and a half shopping days left before Christmas. Each was listening only to the holiday countdown clock in his or her head.

"Have *you* stopped fantasizing about having sex with Freddie Prinze Jr. and Jake Gyllenhaal at the same time?" she countered.

"Hey, *that* could actually happen," Kate said with a smirk. "It's at least possible. Unlike the chance that you, Miss Congeniality, would actually go all Bobbitt on a guy's ass, even if he does totally deserve it."

It wasn't Jude's ass she wanted to…Bobbit. She knew, however, that Kate was right. Lucy wasn't the violent type, except in her fantasies. She might have fun playing a mental game of *why-I-oughta* but she knew nothing would come of it.

"Can't I at least wallow and scheme for an hour?"

"Sure. But we should've done it over beer or tequila in a dive bar. Coffee in a crowded shop just doesn't lend itself to wallowing and scheming."

True. Especially now that this place was no longer the same quiet, cozy hangout she'd loved since coming to New York three and a half years ago. It had once been her favorite place to meet up with friends, do some homework, or just enjoy the silence amid the scent of freshly ground arabica beans.

Since a recent renovation, though, it had turned from a cute, off-the-beaten-track coffee bar into a crazed, credit-card magnet, filled with overpriced gift books, calendars and stationery. Driven city dwellers who excelled at multitasking were flocking to the place to kill two birds with one stone. They could buy a last minute gift for Great-Aunt Susie—a ridiculously overpriced coffee table book titled *The Private Lives of Garden Gnomes,* perhaps—while they waited for their Lite Pomegranate Vanilla Oolang Tea Lattes with whip.

Christmas had been reduced to expedience, kitsch and trendy drinks. Fortunately for her, she'd dropped out of the holiday a few years ago and had no intention of dropping back in.

"Face it, girlfriend, revenge just ain't your style. You're as violent as a Smurf." Kate grinned. "Or one of Santa's elves."

"Not funny," Lucy said, rolling her eyes. "*So* not funny."

Her friend knew how much she disliked the silly costume she had to wear for her "internship" with a local photographer. Intern? Ha. She was a ridiculously dressed *unpaid* Christmas elf wiping the drool off kids' chins as they sat on Santa's lap. What could be more sad to someone who dreamed of being a serious photographer? Someone who was leaving to study abroad in Paris next month, and hoped to go back there to live after graduation? Someone who planned to spend the next several years shooting her way across Europe, one still image at a time?

That girl shouldn't care about Jude. That girl *didn't* care about Jude.

But at this moment, Lucy didn't feel like that girl. For all the violent fantasies, what *this* girl felt right now was hurt.

"You know, for the life of me, I still can't figure out why I ever went out with him in the first place." She swallowed, hard. "I should have known better."

Kate's smirk faded and she reached over to squeeze Lucy's hand. Kate had been witness to what had been Lucy's most humiliating moment ever. Said moment being when Lucy had let herself in to her boyfriend Jude's apartment, to set up his big surprise birthday party that was scheduled for tonight.

Surprise! Your boyfriend is a lying, cheating asshat!

Jude had already gotten started on his birthday celebration. Contrary to his claim that he was going to "pop in" on his family for the day, Jude had apparently decided to stay in town and pop in on his neighbor's vagina.

At least, that's who Lucy thought had been kneeling in front of the sofa with Jude's johnson in her mouth when she and Kate had walked into the apartment. She couldn't be certain. They only saw the back of the bare-ass naked woman's head—oh, plus her bare ass and, uh, the rest of her nether regions. *Ew, ew, ew.* She was still fighting the urge to thrust two coffee stirrers into her eyes to gouge out the image burned onto her retinas. If she'd ever had any doubt she was strictly hetero, her response to that sight would have removed it.

"Maybe I should ask Teddy to beat him up."

Teddy, Kate's boyfriend, was as broad as a table, and could snap Jude like a twig. There was just one problem. "He's more of a pacifist than I am," Lucy said with a smile, knowing Kate had intended to make her laugh. Teddy was the sweetest guy on the planet. "Besides, we both know Jude's not worth the trouble."

"No, he's not." Then Kate grinned. "I am glad you got off a couple of good zingers, though. I still can't believe you asked him if the store was out of birthday candles and that's why he'd found something else that needed to be blown."

That, she had to admit, had been a pretty good line. It was a rare occurrence; the kind of one-liner she usually would have thought of hours later, when reliving the awful experience in her mind. Though, in this instance, since she was now feeling more sad than anything else, she might have been picturing herself asking him why he'd felt the need to be so deceitful.

If he'd told her it wasn't working out and he wanted to see other people, would she have been devastated?

No. A little disappointed, probably, but not crushed.

But to be cheated on—and to walk in on it? *That* rankled.

"Of course, I wouldn't have been able to speak. I'da been busy ripping the extensions outta that ho's head," Kate added.

"She didn't cheat on me, Jude did." Then, curious, she asked, "How do you know they were extensions?"

"Honey, that carpet *so* didn't match those drapes."

Though a peal of laughter emerged from her mouth, Lucy also groaned and threw a hand over her eyes, wishing for a bleach eye-wash. "Don't remind me!"

Funny that she could actually manage to laugh.

Maybe that said a lot about where her feelings for Jude had really been. This girlfriend-gripe session wasn't so much about Lucy's broken heart as it was her disappointed expectations.

She'd really wanted Jude to be a nice guy. A good guy.

Face it, you just wanted someone *in your life.*

Maybe that was true. Seeing the former man-eater Kate so happy was inspiring. But her brother Sam's recent engagement had also really affected her. Their tiny family unit—made even tinier when they'd been left alone in the world after the deaths of their parents—was going to change. Sam had found someone, he was forming a new family, one she'd always be welcome in but wasn't actually a major part of.

She'd wanted something like that, too. Or at least the possibility of something like that, someday. Heck, maybe deep down she also just hadn't wanted to haul her virginity along with her to Europe, and had been hoping she'd finally found the guy who would truly inspire her to shuck it.

Yes, that was probably why she'd let down her guard and gotten involved with Jude when she'd known he wasn't the right one in the long run. Being totally honest, she knew she was more sad at the idea of losing the boyfriend than at losing the actual guy. Not to mention continuing to carry the virgin mantle around her neck.

"Well, at least you didn't sleep with him!" said Kate, who'd had more lovers than Lucy had had birthdays.

"I'll drink to that," she said, sipping her coffee, meaning it. Because being stuck with a hymen was better than having let somebody so rotten remove it.

Something inside her must have recognized that about him, and held her back. Deep down she'd known there was something wrong about the relationship, even though he'd gone out of his way to make it seem so very right.

Maybe Lucy really was the oldest living virgin in New York—kept that way throughout high school by her bad-ass older brother's reputation, and throughout college out of her own deep-rooted romantic streak. Whatever the reason, she'd waited this long. So, as much as she wanted to know what all the fuss was about, she hadn't been about to leap into bed with Jude just because he'd said he liked her photography and opened the door for her when they went out, unlike most other college-aged dudes she knew.

Good thing. Because it had all been an act. The nice, patient, tender guy didn't exist. Jude had put on that persona the way somebody else might don a Halloween costume, sliding into it to be the man she wanted, then taking it off—along with the rest of his clothes— when she wasn't around. He shouldn't be studying to be an attorney, an actor would be much more appropriate. God, could she have been any more gullible?

Maybe Sam was right. Maybe she really had no business living on her own in New York or, worse, going off to Europe. Perhaps she was a lamb in the midst of wolves. She should've just stayed in the Chicago suburb where they'd grown up, gone to community college, done first-communion portraits at Sears, married a nice local guy and gotten to work on producing cousins for Sam's future kids. At least then she wouldn't be sitting here all sad at being cheated on by someone she'd hoped was Prince Charming.

"More like King Creeper," she muttered.

"Huh?"

"Nothing. Just thinking about Jude."

Kate nodded, frowned and muttered, "Why are most men jerks? Other than Teddy, of course."

"Your guess is as good as mine."

"There have to be other decent men out there, right?"

"Sam's one," Lucy admitted. "And my Dad sure was."

"Mine is, too." Kate frowned in thought. "Your father managed a car dealership, didn't he?"

"Yes."

"And your brother, Sam, is a cop. My dad's in sales, and Teddy's a trucker. Hmm."

"Your point being?"

Kate tapped the tip of her finger on her mouth. "Most of the guys you've dated have been like Jude. Rich, future attorneys, politicians, doctors…and dickheads, one and all."

Lucy nodded, conceding the point.

"And that's the type I dated, before I met Teddy."

She started to get the picture. "Ahh."

"So maybe you need to look for an everyday guy, who works hard for a living, hasn't had everything handed to him."

That sounded ideal. Unfortunately Lucy couldn't remember the last time she'd met anyone like that. They sure didn't seem to be on the campus of NYU.

"A guy who's so hot he makes you stick to your chair when you watch his muscles bunch under his sweaty T-shirt as he works," Kate said, sounding lost in thought. She was staring past Lucy, as if visualizing this blue collar stud-muffin. "Who knows what to do with his hands, and has enough self-confidence that he doesn't have to show off in front of a woman."

Not used to Kate being so descriptive—but definitely liking the description—Lucy could only nod.

"Somebody like *him*."

This time, Kate's stare was pointed and her gaze speculative. Surprised, Lucy quickly turned to look over her shoulder, toward the front corner of the shop, and saw the *him* in question.

And oh, wow, what a him.

He was young—in his early twenties, probably, like her. But he didn't look much like the guys she interacted with on a daily basis at school. He had on a pair of faded, worn jeans, that hung low on his very lean hips. They were tugged down even further by the work belt he wore over them, which was weighted with various tools. Powerful hammers, long screwdrivers, steely drills. All hard. Strong. Stiff.

Get your mind out of his toolbelt.

She did, shaking her head quickly to get her attention going in another direction. Of course, there wasn't any other direction to go…he was hot any way you looked at it.

So she looked at it. Er, him.

Lucy lifted her gaze, taking in the whole tall, lean, powerful package. Though he wore the tools of the trade, he was not built like a brawny construction-worker type. Strong, yes, but with a youthful leanness—Hugh Jackman as Leopold, not as Wolverine.

Yum.

His entire body told tales of hard work An impressive set of abs rippled visibly beneath the sweat-tinged

T-shirt. His broad chest and thickly muscled arms moved with almost poetic precision as he finished installing a new bookcase in the back corner of the shop.

He lifted one arm and wiped a sheen of sweat off his forehead, which just emphasized the handsomeness of his face, seen only in profile. He had a strong, square jaw, a straight nose. High cheekbones emphasized the lightly stubbled hollows below, lending his lean face an air of youth and power.

His light brown hair was longish, a little shaggy, and he swept it back from his brow with an impatient hand. Seeing the strong hands in motion made Lucy let out a long, slow breath, and when he turned around and she beheld him from the back, she had to suck in another one. Oh, my, did the man know how to fill out a pair of jeans.

Apparently she wasn't the only woman who'd noticed. What she'd taken for shopper's distraction earlier she now realized had been female appreciation for the beautiful display of raw, powerful male in the corner. Every other woman in the place was either sneaking peeks or outright gaping.

She was a gaper. No peeking about it.

Finally realizing she was literally turned in her seat to stare, and probably had drool dripping down her chin, she swung back around to face Kate. Her friend wore a similar expression. "Wow," she admitted.

"Double wow. If I didn't love Teddy, I'd be over there offering to take care of his *tool* for him."

Lucy couldn't help being wicked when she was around Kate. "I bet it could use some lubrication."

"Atta girl!"

"But I think you'd have to stand in line."

"With you?" Kate asked, her eyes sparkling.

Lucy shook her head. "I don't think so. Cheated on and heartbroken an hour ago, remember?"

"Well, cheated on, anyway," said Kate, perceptive as always.

"Touché," Lucy admitted, not terribly surprised to realize she was already feeling better. What had felt like heartbreak ninety minutes ago had segued into a heart cramp. Now it was barely a heart twinge.

Kate glanced at her empty cup, and at Lucy's. "One more?"

"Sure."

"I got it," the other woman said, grabbing her bag. She stood up and walked toward the counter near the front of the shop.

Lucy sighed deeply, then forced herself to put Jude out of her mind. Time to forget about him. He hadn't been her lover, merely a boyfriend who'd gotten a hand down her pants just once in three months. Absolutely forgettable.

Besides which, she had other things to think about. Like Christmas, now just two days away. And the fact that she was spending it alone.

Your own fault. She'd made the choice. Kate was going away with Teddy tonight so the apartment would be empty. But Sam had begged her to come back to Chicago to celebrate Christmas with his fiancée's family. Lucy had refused, claiming she had too much work to do over the holidays.

Truth was, she couldn't handle a big family Christmas. The last traditional holiday season she'd experienced had been a week before her parents had been swept from her life by a stupid asshole who'd decided to celebrate a promotion by having a few bourbons, then getting behind the wheel of a car.

It had been just her and Sam for five years now, and each Christmas had been more nontraditional than the last. One year ago, they'd been in Mexico, lying on a beach, ignoring the merriment around them in favor of rum drinks and steel drums.

Though Sam was ready to dive back into the holiday spirit with his new fiancée, somehow, Lucy just couldn't face it yet. Honestly, she wasn't sure she'd ever be able to again. Christmas had once been her favorite holiday; it seemed almost sacrilege to enjoy it without the two people who had made it so special for the first seventeen years of her life.

Now she had another thing to add to her why-I-should-skip Christmas list: she'd been cheated on—right before the holiday. The angel on the top of Jude's tree had borne witness to the extension-wearing ho who went around sucking on dicks that belonged to other girls. Er, other girls' boyfriends.

"The whole holiday is just overrated," she told herself. "Better off just forgetting about it."

Not to mention a few other things. Like love. Romance.

And men.

"EXCUSE ME, SIR, can I ask you a favor?"

Ross Marshall heard a young woman speaking, but since he knew she wasn't talking to him, he didn't bother turning around. He instead remained focused on putting the finishing touches on the custom-made bookcase he'd been asked to install today. Thankfully, despite his concerns about the off-kilter walls in this old New York building, every shelving unit he'd built for Beans & Books had fit beautifully. Including this last one.

"Sir?"

Though curious, since the voice sounded a little insistent, again he ignored her. He tried to avoid the customers and usually didn't work until later in the evening when the shop was closed. The owner really wanted the final unit installed today, however—gotta have more shelf space to grab those crazy day-before-Christmas-Eve shoppers who'd be filling the aisles tonight. So he'd agreed to come in right after the frenetic lunch hour but before the five o'clock rush.

He'd still arrived just in time to listen to modern-day robber barons having power coffees while making let's-take-over-the-world deals via Bluetooth. Oh, and their trophy wives stopping by between Junior League meetings and museum openings to grab a Fat-Free Cappuccino with Soy milk and carob drizzle.

Manhattan was like a different planet. He preferred Chicago, which he'd called home for the first twenty-three of his twenty-four years. It was almost as big and half as pretentious.

"Hellooooo?"

Finally realizing the woman might actually be speaking to him, which he hadn't imagined since in New York nobody called hammer jockeys "sir," he turned around. The young woman *had* been addressing him—she was staring at him, her eyes narrowed, her freckled cheeks flushed and her mouth tugged down into a frown.

"I'm sorry, I didn't realize you were talking to me."

He offered her a smile. "I'm not used to being called sir."

The blonde relaxed. "Oh, yeah. Sorry. Hey, listen, could I ask you a big favor?"

He stiffened the tiniest bit. He might not be used to being called sir around here, but he'd received a lot of suggestive invitations lately. It seemed men with calluses were, for some reason, catnip to the rich Manhattan types. "Yes?"

"See my friend over there at the table in the far corner?"

Ross glanced over, seeing the back of a woman seated in the shadowy rear corner of the place. Then he looked again, interested despite himself in the stunning, thick brown hair that fell in loose, curly waves halfway down her back. She stood out from every other female in the place—most of whom sported a more typical, reserved, New York professional-woman's blow-out or bun. Ross's hands started to tingle, as if anticipating what it might be like to sink his fingers into those silky strands.

He shoved them into his pockets. "What about her?"

"She's my best friend—we're both students. Anyway, she needs some help for this project she's working on. We've been sitting over there talking about it and trying to figure out what tool would be best." She lifted her shoulders in a shrug. "But we're both pretty clueless about that kind of stuff. Do you think you could go over and offer her your expertise?"

It sounded screwy to him, and the young woman looked like she was about to break into a grin. But something—*that hair*—made him curious to see more of the girl with the tool problem.

He looked again. This time, the brunette had turned a little, as if looking around for her friend, and he caught a glimpse of her face. Creamy-skin. Cute nose. Long lashes. Full mouth.

His heart-rate kicked up a notch; he was interested in spite of himself. "What kind of job is it?" he asked as he began to pack up his portable toolbox.

"Well, uh…it might be best if she explains that herself." As if sensing he was skeptical, she added, "She's a photography student, you see, and I'm in journalism. Between the two of us, we barely know the difference between a hammer and a chainsaw."

He shouldn't. Really. Even though he was finished here, he had some things to do for another project scheduled to start the day after Christmas. He needed to phone in a few orders, go to the lumberyard, go over the design he'd sketched out.

Of course, all that would have to come after he risked life and limb at the most miserable place on earth to be today: the nearest shipping store. He had to get his family's Christmas gifts sent off, via overnight delivery, obviously. Seemed in the past week he had gone from busy self-employed carpenter to forgetful procrastinating shopper. Bad enough that he wasn't going home for Christmas; if he didn't get a gift in front of his youngest sister, he'd never hear the end of it.

Yet even with all that, he was tempted to take ten minutes to see if the brunette was really as attractive as she looked from here. Not to mention seeing what this mystery project was.

"Please? I'm sure it won't take long. Besides, helping someone else will put you in the holiday spirit," the girl said, managing to sound pious, despite the mischief in her expression.

He chuckled at her noble tone. Her smile and the twinkle in her eyes told him something else was going on. She was probably playing some kind of matchmaking game. Hell, for all he knew, the brunette had put her up to this, wanting to meet him but not wanting to come on too strong.

That was okay. Because he suddenly wanted to meet her, too.

And if the blonde was on the up-and-up, and the woman did need some help, well, that was okay, too. Maybe doing something nice for someone—someone super hot with soft-looking hair he wanted to rub all over his bare skin—was just what he needed. Certainly nothing else was putting him in the holiday spirit. He was too busy working—trying to prove to himself and to everyone else that he could make it on his own and didn't need to go to work in the family business—to care much about celebrating.

His mom suspected that was why he wasn't coming home for Christmas, because he didn't want to get another guilt trip or have another argument with his dad. She wasn't entirely wrong.

"Okay," he said, seeing the shop owner smiling broadly at him from behind the counter, obviously thrilled that even more expensive holiday junk could be shoveled in front of potential customers within the hour. "Just give me a few minutes."

"Oh, thank you!"

The freckled blonde turned and headed not for her friend in the back corner, but toward the door of the shop. Like she was making herself scarce so her friend could make her move. He grinned, wondering why girls went through these motions. He would probably have been even more interested if the brunette had just come up to him herself and said hello.

Finishing up with a customer, the owner came out from around the counter. He offered Ross his exuberant thanks for having squeezed in this job so quickly. Ross accepted the check for final payment—which, he noted, included a nice holiday bonus—then shook the man's hand and picked up his tools. Then it was decision time. Head for the exit and get busy doing what he needed to do? Or take a few minutes out of his day to possibly be hit-on by a very pretty girl who'd gotten her friend to play matchmaker?

Hell. He might be hungry, might need work to pay his bills. But he was twenty-four, human and male. Pretty girl trumped food any day of the week.

Heading toward her table, he brushed some sawdust off his arms, nodding politely at the several women who smiled and murmured holiday greetings. The brunette hadn't moved from her seat, though he did see her look from side to side, as if she wanted to turn around to see if he was coming over, but didn't wish to be too obvious about it.

She so *set this up.*

Frankly, Ross couldn't bring himself to care.

He walked up behind her, about to clear his throat and introduce himself, when he heard her say something. She was alone, obviously, and had to be talking to herself. And what she said pierced a hole in the ego that had been telling him she'd sent a friend over to get his attention.

"You know you'd have been scared to even pick up a chainsaw," she muttered. "Or even an electric knife!"

Damn. She really was talking about tools? Some project that she needed to do?

Ross had to laugh at himself. Wouldn't his youngest sister—always his biggest critic—be laughing her ass off right now? He'd been all cocky and sure this sexy coed was about to come on to him…and she really was interested only in his toolbelt.

"Forget the electric knife," he said, intruding on her musings, the carpenter in him shuddering at the thought. "They're not made for cutting anything other than meat."

The girl swung her head up to look at him, her eyes rounding in shock and her mouth dropping open.

Big brown eyes. Full, pink-lipped mouth.

Then there was the perfect, heart-shaped face. And oh, that hair. Thick and shining, with soft brown waves that framed her face, and curls that tumbled well down her back. There wasn't a guy alive who wouldn't imagine all that hair being the only thing wrapped around her naked body; well, except for his *own* naked body.

He stared, unable to do anything else. She'd been pretty from across the room. Up close, she was beautiful enough to make his heart forget it was supposed to beat.

"Excuse me?" she said, shaking her head lightly as if she couldn't figure out what was happening. "What did you say?"

He cleared his throat. "I said, you need to use the right tool for the job. Electric knives are for cutting meat. Now what is it you were thinking about cutting through?"

"Meat," she replied, then quickly clamped her lips shut.

He laughed, admiring her quick wit. "Beef or pork?"

"I'd say pork loin," she replied, her mouth twisting a bit. "But I was joking. I definitely don't need to cut any meat."

"I figured," he said. Without waiting for an invitation, he walked around the table and sat in the vacant chair, facing her. He told himself it was because he'd promised her friend he'd offer her some construction advice. In truth, he just wanted to look at her a little more. Hear her voice. See whether she had a personality to go with the looks.

Most guys his age probably wouldn't care. Ross, though, did.

He might be young, but he wasn't inexperienced. And he'd learned very early on that a pretty face and smoking-hot body were enough before hitting the sheets. But after that, if there wasn't a great sense of humor, big heart and a brain to go along with the sexiness, he just couldn't stay interested. Some of his old college buddies used to joke about being happy with tits-on-a-stick. Ross preferred a real woman, from top to bottom.

She seemed like she had a brain. Right now, though, he was wondering about that whole personality thing. Because she just kept staring at him, her face turning pink, as if she didn't know what to say.

Or she was embarrassed.

Hmm. So maybe this wasn't about some mystery project. Because the way she was blushing made him suspect she'd had something wicked on her mind.

More interesting by the minute.

"So, what is this big project?"

"Project?"

"Yeah. Your friend came over, told me you needed some advice on tools for a project you're doing."

She sucked her bottom lip into her mouth and closed her eyes for a second, then whispered, "I'm going to kill her."

"Maybe that's why she left—she needed a running start."

"She *left?*"

"Yep. Right after she came to ask me to help you."

Groaning, she shook her head. "I can't believe this."

"So, she was trying to set us up?"

"I think so."

"What kind of friend does that?" he asked. "She doesn't know me—what if I'm some kind of serial killer or panty thief?"

Her brow went up. "Are you?"

"Am I what?"

"Either of those things?"

He grinned. "No on the first. I'll take the fifth on the second until we get to know each other." Certain he wanted that—to get to know her—he stuck out his hand. "I'm Ross."

She eyed it, then reached out and shook. Her hand was small, soft. Fragile against his own. Having worked only with his hands for months, he knew he had calluses on top of blisters, but she didn't seem to mind at all. In fact, she was the one who held on for a moment, as if not wanting to let go.

Finally, though, she pulled away, murmuring, "Lucy."

"Nice to meet you, Lucy."

"You, too. Especially now that I know you're not a serial killer." She flashed a grin. "As for the other, remind me not to walk into Victoria's Secret with you... wouldn't want to get arrested as an accomplice."

"What fun would there be in stealing brand-new panties?" Then, seeing her brow shoot up, he held up a hand. "Kidding. Believe me, stealing underwear isn't my thing."

"Helping mystery girls with mysterious projects is?"

"Uh-huh. Now, mysterious girl, back to the mysterious project."

"There isn't one."

"Your friend made it up?"

She shifted her gaze, those long lashes lowering. "Not exactly. I was, um, wondering which tool to use to, uh, remove something. And she obviously thought it would be fun to bring you into my fantasies." She gasped, staring him in the eye. "I mean, I wasn't...it's not that I was fantasizing about you!"

"Aww, I'm crushed."

"If you knew the fantasy, you wouldn't be," she said, her tone droll.

"So why don't you tell me?" he asked, only half-teasing. What *did* a beautiful young woman fantasize about? More importantly, *who?*

"Believe me, you don't want to know."

"Oh, trust me on this, I definitely do."

She studied him for a moment, eyeing him intently as if to see if he was serious. Then, apparently realizing he was, she came right out and told him.

3

JUST BECAUSE ROSS MARSHALL hadn't seen Lucy Fleming for six years did not mean he didn't instantly recognize her. It did, however, mean his heart literally thudded in his chest and his brain seemed to flatline. The huge, open reception area of his office—decorated with lights and greenery—seemed to darken. It also appeared to shrink, squeezing in tight, crushing his ribs, making his head throb, sending him off-kilter. He couldn't form a single coherent thought.

Well, maybe one. *You cut your hair?* He had the presence of mind to notice that the long, riotous curls that had once fallen well down her back had been tamed and shortened. Then everything just went blank.

She couldn't be here, right? Could not *possibly* be here. This had to be a dream—he was still sleeping and she was visiting his nighttime fantasies, as she so often had over the years.

He couldn't resist, needing to grab the moment

before he woke up. He lifted a hand, put it on her shoulder, felt the solid, real person beneath the elf costume. She didn't immediately pull away, and he leaned a little bit closer, breathing deeply, recognizing the scent that was uniquely Lucy. Not a perfume or a lotion or her shampoo. Just something distinctive and evocative that called to his memories, reminding him that she had been *the one*.

And he'd let her get away.

"You're not dreaming," she told him, her tone dry.

He dropped his hand and stepped back, needing to get his head back in the game. "Guess that means you're not, either."

"That thought did cross my mind," she said, her big brown eyes inquisitive. "I certainly never expected to run into you, today of all days."

He knew the day. Knew it well. Which just made the meeting all the more surreal. "Same here," he mumbled.

They both fell silent. Lucy appeared as stunned as he was.

Well, why wouldn't she be? They hadn't laid eyes on each other in years. Despite what had happened between them, what they'd shared over that one amazing holiday season, not one word had been exchanged between them since mid-January, nearly six years ago. Not a card, not a phone call. No chance of bumping into each other since, the last he'd known, she had been bound for Europe.

But here she was. Not just in Chicago, but in his office.

His freaking office!

"What are you doing here?" he asked, his brain not

catching up yet. It should be obvious. Lucy had been studying photography when they'd met. Besides which, she was carrying a camera bag. And was dressed as an elf.

A smile tried to tug at his lips. He remembered that elf costume. Remembered it so well.

Suddenly he was remembering everything so well.

Some things *too* well.

"I'm working," she said, her head going up, that pretty mouth tightening. "Did you happen to notice the picture-with-Santa session that's been going on for the past couple of hours?"

He'd barely noticed anything that was going on, being too busy working to socialize. The employee Christmas party had been a long-standing tradition with Elite Construction, the company his grandfather had founded, and he now ran. That didn't mean the boss ever had much time to participate in it. He'd made the rounds, thanked his employees, greeted their kids and wives, then retreated back into his office for the last two hours, only coming out to say goodbye now that things were winding down.

"I noticed," he finally replied.

"Well, that was me behind the camera."

"I know that, I heard you did a great job and was coming over to meet you," he said, still knocked off-kilter by her mere presence.

"Sorry, Santa's gone. No more pictures. Though, if you want to sit on the chair, I guess I could snap a shot of you holding a candy cane and a teddy bear."

Still sassy. God, he'd always liked that about her.

"I meant, I was coming to thank you for agreeing to do the party on such short notice."

"You didn't know *I* was the elf until just now?" she asked, sounding slightly suspicious. As if wondering if he'd set up this little reunion.

Huh. If he'd known she was nearby, he might have considered doing just that—even though Lucy probably wouldn't have been thrilled about it, judging by the look on her face.

"I swear, I had no idea." He was suddenly very interested in talking to his assistant, wondering how she'd found Lucy. He also wondered if the motherly, slightly nosy woman had been doing a little matchmaking. He wouldn't put it past her. She was nothing if not a closet romantic.

"My real question was," he continued, "what are you doing here in Chicago? You swore you'd never live here. Hell, I figured you'd be in Europe."

That had been her dream, living overseas, being a world-traveling photographer. So what had happened? She had seemed utterly determined that she would never stay near home and take…Santa pictures of little kids.

He glanced at the velvet-covered chair, the fluffy fake snow, the tripod, and her, back in that elf suit.

How on earth had her life gotten so derailed?

"I was for a while, did my semester abroad and went back right after graduation," she said.

Just as she'd planned. Which was one reason he'd stayed out of touch, knowing an entire ocean was going to separate them, so why bother trying to make something work when geography said it couldn't?

"And?"

"And I wasn't happy, so I ended up back in New York a few years ago."

Years. She'd been on the same continent for years. A short plane ride away. The thought made him slightly sick to his stomach, especially considering the number of times he'd thought about her during that same time span. The curiosity about whether she'd kept the same cell phone number and whether it would work in Paris.

Maybe not. But it probably would have in New York. Damn.

"How did Chicago enter the equation?"

"You remember, I grew up in this area?"

He remembered, but she'd seemed adamant about never coming back here, associating it with her tragic loss. "I remember."

"Well, I moved back here ten months ago to be closer my brother."

Even as another wave of shocked pleasure washed over him—she'd moved *here,* to the very same city— the brother's name immediately popped into his mind. "Sam?"

"Right. He went through a pretty bad divorce and I thought he could use some family nearby."

"That's a shame…about the divorce, I mean."

"Yes, it is. I really thought they'd make it."

"Does anybody anymore?" he mumbled before he could think better of it.

Her whole body stiffened, and he mentally kicked himself for going there. Because he and Lucy sure hadn't.

Then again, had they expected to? Hell, what had happened between them had been so sudden, so unexpected. Neither of them had been in the right place for any kind of relationship—mentally, emotionally, financially, or in any other way.

Except physically. Oh, yeah. There they'd been absolutely perfect together.

It had been so good during the incredibly brief time it lasted. Honestly, looking back, he could say it was the best Christmas Eve he'd ever had in his life.

Followed by the worst Christmas Day.

"How do you like being back in Chicago?" he asked, sensing she was trying to gracefully exit stage left.

"It's cold," she said with a shrug, not giving an inch, not softening up a bit. Hell, he supposed he couldn't blame her.

"You look like you've done well for yourself," she said, an almost grudging tone to her voice. She looked him over, head-to-toe, as if wondering where the jeans, T-shirt and tool belt had gone.

Some days—many days—he longed for them. Wearing a suit—even if he usually lost the tie and rolled-up his sleeves at some point every day—just didn't excite him the way working with his hands always had. "I guess. And you?"

She nodded. "I have my own studio."

"Still boycott Christmas?"

She glanced down at her costume. "As much as I possibly can, which isn't easy in my line of work. You still a sappy kid about it?"

He nodded, unashamed. "Absolutely." Even if, for the past five holiday seasons, he'd spent a lot more time wondering about Lucy—where she'd gone, if she'd stayed in Europe, become a famous photographer—than he had worrying about what present to get for which sister, niece or nephew.

As if they'd both run out of small talk for the moment, they returned to staring. Ross couldn't deny

it, the years had been good to her; Lucy was beautiful. No perky little elf hat complete with feather could
take away from that. Nor could the short dress, striped
tights—oh, God, those tights, did they ever bring back
memories—and pointy-tipped shoes.

She should look cute and adorable. Instead she
looked hot and sexy, bringing wild, intense memories
to his mind of the last time he'd seen her wearing that
very same outfit.

He was suddenly—forcibly—reminded of how long
it had been since he'd had sex.

Good sex? Even longer.

Fabulous, never-forget-it, once-in-a-lifetime sex?

Six years. No doubt about it.

He swallowed as memories flooded over him,
having to shift a little. Lucy had always affected him
physically. Damned if he wanted anyone to notice that
now, though. The CEO wasn't supposed to sport wood
at the corporate holiday party.

"I'm impressed that you can still fit into that," he admitted against his own better judgment. "But not too
surprised. You haven't changed a bit."

She flushed. "Maybe not physically. But I'm not the
same sweet, wide-eyed kid anymore."

He barked a laugh. "Sweet kid? Aren't you the
same person who was planning to dismember her ex-
boyfriend when we met?"

"I didn't actually *do* it."

No, she hadn't. As he recalled, Ross had enjoyed the
pleasure of taking her ex apart. And it had felt damn
good, too.

"That's good—I'd hate to think you've spent the last
six years in jail."

"Maybe if you hadn't stopped calling, you'd know where I spent the last six years," she replied, ever-so-sweetly.

Direct hit. He winced. "Look, Lucy…"

She waved a hand, obviously angry at herself for having said anything. "Forget it. Water under the bridge."

"You know what I was going through—why I left New York." Of course she knew, she'd been there when he'd gotten the call that brought him back home.

"I know," she said. "I understood…I under*stand*."

Maybe. But that not-staying-in-touch thing obviously still rankled.

He'd probably asked himself a dozen times over the years why he hadn't at least tried to get back in touch with her once his life had returned to something resembling normal. Maybe a hundred times. It always came back to the same thing: he was stuck. His life was here. Hers was…anywhere she wanted it to be. And she'd wanted it to be in another country, and a completely different reality from his, which was filled with contracts and workers-comp issues and the cost of lumber.

She'd been off to capture the world one still image at a time. He'd been boxed in, chained to the past, owing too much to other people to just go and live his life the way he had wanted to.

Not that it had turned out badly. He actually loved running the business and had done a damn fine job of it. He was glad to live in Chicago. He liked the vibe of this city, the people and the culture. So no, he didn't regret coming back here. He had only one regret. Her.

"And now here you are," he murmured, though he hadn't intended to say it out loud.

"Don't make a big thing of it," she insisted. "I had no idea you worked here."

"And if you had known? Would you have taken the job today, risked bumping into me?"

She didn't reply. Which was answer enough.

Lucy really was mad at him. Well, that made two of them; he was mad at himself. Plenty of room for regrets, with six years of what-ifs under his belt. But at the time it had seemed like he was doing the right thing—the best thing—for both of them.

Of course, he'd questioned that just about every day since.

"Excuse me, Ross?"

He glanced away from Lucy, seeing Stella, his administrative assistant, who he'd inherited from *his* father. Who'd inherited her from his father. Older than dirt didn't describe her. She had dirt beat—you'd have to go back to the rocks that had been worn down into the dirt to describe her.

You wouldn't know it to look at her. From the bottled black dye job to the floral-print dress, she could pass for fifty. But Ross knew she'd passed that milestone at least two decades ago. He dreaded the day she was no longer around to keep him organized.

Or to matchmake? He was going to have to have a talk with Stella about that. He knew his assistant thought he was stressed and lonely and spent too much time in the office. Plus, Stella knew about Lucy—she was one of the few people who did, having gotten Ross to reveal the story after one long, stressful day. But would she have gone to that much trouble—tracking Lucy down and getting her here? It seemed crazy.

If it was true, he would have to decide whether to

give her hell for meddling in his private affairs…or thank her.

The way Lucy wasn't bothering to hide her dislike made him suspect the former.

The thought that he might be able to get her to change her mind? Definitely the latter.

He didn't deny he was still interested. Still attracted. Judging by the absence of a ring on her left hand, he suspected she was available—at least technically. So maybe it was time to take his shot. See if he could make up for six wasted years. See if there was any way she could forgive him for walking—no, running—away before they ever really had a chance to get started.

"Ross?" Stella prompted again. "Mr. Whitaker is about to leave, and he'd like to see you before he goes."

Whitaker—a client who'd sent a lot of work their way over the past several years. He wasn't somebody Ross could ignore.

"Okay," he said, before turning his attention back to Lucy. "Wait for me." It wasn't a request.

"No, I really have to go. It was nice to see you."

Said like she'd say it was nice to see an elementary school bully she'd loathed for decades. Damn. He'd screwed this up so badly. Six years ago, and today.

"Lucy, please…"

"Uh, Miss Fleming? If you'd step into the office, I can get you your payment right away," Stella interjected. "I'm sure you'd prefer not to have to wait until after the holidays."

Her lush bottom lip snagged between her teeth, Lucy looked torn. Ross glanced at Stella, wondering if she was intentionally using some stalling tactics to keep Lucy around. Then again, if she'd been trying to set them up, she probably wouldn't have interrupted about Whitaker, no matter how important a client he was. So maybe this whole thing had just been luck. Good luck. Incredibly good luck.

And maybe it meant he was going to have another chance with the woman he'd so foolishly let slip away.

HMM. MONEY OR DIGNITY? Go with the bossy assistant, or run like hell? *Decisions, decisions.*

Normally Lucy would have been heading toward the door the second Ross's back was turned. She had work to do, editing, photoshopping, cropping…plus all the stuff a small business owner was responsible for, but which often slipped through the cracks when the customers kept walking steadily through the door.

They wouldn't be walking through the door on Christmas weekend, though, so she should be able to catch up. And one thing she needed to catch up on was ordering. She had some equipment to buy, and paying for it by December 31 would make her tax bill a lot lighter come spring.

Which meant she should really stick around for the money. They'd offered her a *lot,* both for her time, and for the portrait packages the company had preordered for every family. It might even be enough money to get the new laptop *and* the new lens she needed.

Ross stared at her, not pleading, not ordering. Just asking her to wait, give them a chance to talk. To catch up on old times? Seriously, what was there to say except, *Hey, remember that time we had crazy wild sex in a pile of fluff in Santa's workshop?*

Good times.

Times that would never be repeated.

"I really should go," she said.

The administrator, who had a brusque manner that said she didn't like to take no for an answer, didn't take no for an answer. "Don't be silly, it won't take five minutes. It will save our accountants some trouble."

She eyed the woman doubtfully, suspecting this place did not keep their receipts and canceled checks in empty Amazon.com boxes the way she did.

"After the party, the offices shut down until New Year's. So I'd really like to get this taken care of today, clear the party off the books, if you will."

Huh. Sounded like every business had to deal with that pesky little IRS thing, even businesses as big as this one. Which, judging by the size of this brand-new six-story office building, and the fact that Elite Construction took up every floor of it, was very big, indeed. She wondered again what Ross did here. Obviously he no longer swung a hammer—he was dressed like a corporate guy.

She couldn't help wondering what had happened to his dream of someday buying a piece of property and building a house on it, every stone, every shutter, every plank of wood put there with his own hands. Had Ross given up his dreams? Or had they merely changed, like hers had?

As if realizing his presence was making her reluctant, Ross said, "I should go. It was great seeing you again, Lucy."

"You, too."

She forced a tight smile, wishing she could hit Rewind and go back a half hour to think of something else to say to this man. Something breezy and casual, something that wouldn't have revealed how she felt about not hearing from him after that one magical holiday. Something *other* than, "Well, if you'd called, you'd know where I'd been for the past six years."

Weak, girl. So weak. She could almost hear Kate's voice scolding her for making that snotty, hurt-sounding comment. Even though, now, there would be echoes of a baby and a toddler crying in the background as they had the conversation. Kate had married Teddy and started repopulating the planet.

Lucy, meanwhile, had managed only sexual affairs after Ross. But she hadn't come anywhere close to falling in love. Not after the one-two punch she'd taken at twenty-two. First Jude, then Ross—the latter being the one who'd truly taught her about love and loss. Her poor heart had formed an exoskeleton thicker than an insect's. Since then, she'd made love 'em and leave 'em a way of life, only substituting the *love* with *do*.

Even Kate had been impressed.

She watched him walk away, noting that he didn't look back. His departure should have made it easier to stick around for a few minutes to get paid. Instead it just pissed her off. Ross was always the one who got to walk away. One of these days she wanted to be the one to make the grand exit.

But grand exits didn't buy lenses and laptops. Money did. She'd spent a lot moving her studio from New York to Chicago. Yes, she was building a reputation and business was good. This one check, though, could do some nice things for her bottom line.

If she deposited the check tonight, then by this weekend, she could be happily shopping for laptops online while everybody else in the world unwrapped ugly sweaters and ate rock-hard fruitcake. She had bookings lined up all next week—a few of them big ones that could lead to some serious money. Plus, she was hoping to hear from a children's magazine in New York, to whom she'd submitted some work. She wanted to be ready if they called and said they wanted more.

"Okay, if you can pay me now, I'd really appreciate it," she finally told the administrator, who'd been waiting patiently, watching Lucy watch Ross.

"Excellent, come along."

Lucy put down her camera and lens bags, and followed the woman, who'd introduced herself as Stella when she'd called a week ago to hire her. They left the party behind, heading down a long corridor toward the executive offices. Lucy couldn't help noticing the opulence of this area, the thick carpet sinking beneath her feet, the beautiful artwork lining the walls. Somebody had spent a lot of time decorating this place and she suspected their clients ranked among Chicago's most wealthy.

At the back end of the executive wing was an enclosed suite, into which Stella led her. A broad receptionist's desk stood in the middle of a waiting area, blocking access to an imposing set of double doors. Stella breezed through them, into what looked like the head honcho's office. It was huge, a corner room with floor-to-ceiling windows on two walls. The building wasn't terribly high, but the location right on the water on the very outskirts of town meant nothing interrupted the beautiful view. The desk was as big as the kitchen in her tiny apartment, and in a partially blocked-off alcove, she saw an area for relaxation, complete with a refrigerator, TV and a fold-out couch...folded out.

"Wow, is your boss a slave-driver? Do you have to be on call 24/7?"

The woman glanced around, then realized what Lucy was talking about. "That's just for him. Our CEO is only hard on himself."

"Does he live here or something?"

"It sometimes seems that way," Stella said. "When we moved into this new building, he was spending so many hours here, I ordered the couch and make it up for him when I suspect he'll pull an all-nighter."

"That's dedication." On Stella's part, and on her boss's.

"It's paid off. Elite is thriving when new construction is down nationwide."

"I could tell by the party," she admitted, knowing it must have set the company back a pretty penny. Few corporations bothered these days, and she suspected the happy atmosphere contributed to the company's success.

Stella stepped behind the desk and picked up a pile of sealed envelopes, shuffling through a half-dozen of them before she said, "Ah, here we are!"

Lucy accepted it, tucking the very welcome check into her purse. "Thanks very much."

"Thank *you*. Your photos were the hit of the party. I am actually glad the other company canceled. We've used them in the past and they've never had the response you did today. You're wonderful with children."

Lucy smiled, appreciating the praise. It was funny— six years ago, she probably would have been horrified at it.

Honestly, she wasn't sure herself how it had happened. She just knew that, after two years in Paris, photographing cold-faced fashion models had lost all appeal. Same with old, lifeless buildings and stagnant landscapes.

Then Kate had started having kids. Lucy had visited for summers and holidays, be ming a devoted god-mother and falling head-ove eels for those babies. She had delighted in taking their portraits, finding in children's faces an energy and spontaneity she seldom found anywhere else.

So she'd gone back to New York. She'd set up a studio and begun exploring the amazingly creative world of little people. One thing had led to another, and then another. And soon she'd been getting calls from wealthy parents in other states, and had sold several shots to children's catalogs and magazines.

Who'd've ever thought it?

Not her, that's for sure. Nor would she ever have imagined that she'd really love what she was doing. But she did.

Life, it seemed, took some strange turns, led you in directions you'd never have imagined. It had taken her from the windy city, to the Big Apple, then to another continent. And now right back to where she'd started, in Chicago.

And back into Ross Marshall's life.

No, don't even go there, she reminded herself. She wasn't back in his life. She was in the same building with him for another five minutes, max. Then she could go back to forgetting about the guy. Forgetting how good he still looked to her. How his sexy voice thrilled her senses. How his touch had sent her out of her mind.

How he'd once seemed like the guy she could love forever.

4

LUCY HAD TO GIVE THIS very handsome stranger—
Ross—credit. He didn't stand up and walk out of the
coffee shop when she admitted she'd been fantasizing about separating an ex-boyfriend from part of his
anatomy. He didn't yelp, cringe, or reflexively drop a
protective hand on his lap. None of the above. Instead
he simply stared for a second, then let a loud burst of
laughter erupt from his mouth.

She smiled, too, especially because she hadn't *really*
been fantasizing about maiming Jude when this guy
had walked up behind her. In fact, she'd been laughing
at herself for having thought about it earlier. Somehow,
her whole mood had shifted from the time she'd walked
into the coffee shop until the moment this incredibly
handsome man had approached her.

Incredibly. Handsome.

Around them, others in the café glanced over. Lucy
wasn't blind to the stares that lingered on him. Heaven

knew, any woman with a broken-in vagina would stare. Heck, hers wasn't broken-in and she could barely take her eyes off the guy!

He'd been super-hot from across the room. Up close, now that she could see the tiny flecks in his stunning green eyes, the dazzling white smile, the slight stubble on his cheeks, well, he went from hot and sexy to smoking and irresistible. She'd actually shivered when their hands had met, unable to think a single thought except to wonder how those strong, rough fingers would feel sliding across her skin.

Gorgeous, sexy, strong. And a sense of humor.

Why couldn't she have met this guy on a day when she didn't loathe every creature with a penis?

You don't. Not every guy.

Truthfully? Not even one. She didn't loathe Jude. She would have had to care about him to hate him, and, honestly, having really thought about it, she knew she hadn't cared much at all.

"You're serious?" he asked once his laughter had died down.

"Not about doing it."

"But thinking it?"

"My turn to take the fifth."

"Why?"

"Probably because it's not very nice to admit you fantasize about dismembering someone."

"No, I meant why do you want to, um…dismember him?"

"I didn't, I was just indulging in a little mind-revenge. He wasn't the most faithful guy."

"I hate cheaters," he said, his voice both sympathetic and disgusted.

"Speaking from personal experience?"

"Well, not exactly," he admitted.

Yeah. Because any woman who cheated on him would have to have been recently lobotomized.

"Though, I did kinda get cheated on once…by a guy."

She didn't take the bait, knowing that there was no way Ross was gay. There wasn't one nonheterosexual gene in his body; you could practically smell the masculine pheromones that surrounded him like a cloud, attracting every woman in the place.

"Let me guess…your best buddy in first grade decided he wanted to play dodgeball instead of tag and left you alone in the playground?"

"Almost," he said, his eyes gleaming with approval that she hadn't gone where most would have. "It was in high school. I wanted my best friend to stick with the wrestling team, he wanted to do the school musical." He shook his head sadly. "I just couldn't understand what he was thinking. It wasn't until junior year that he finally told me the truth, and then I was so furious I didn't speak to him for a week."

Somehow disappointed in him, she stiffened slightly. "You were mad that he was gay?"

"Hell, no, he wasn't gay! He told me he left wrestling and went to drama because, let me see if I remember this exactly, 'Why would I want to roll around on the floor with a bunch of sweaty dudes, when I could be one of only a handful of guys surrounded by some of the prettiest girls in the school?' Man, some of those theater chicks were cute…and he never told me, he kept them all for himself!"

She laughed out loud, liking both the story, and that

he had told it. He was obviously trying to distract her, to amuse her. It was a nice thing to do for a guy so young and good-looking.

"So, your first bro-mance ended up in a bad breakup."

"Yup. Now, back to yours...."

"Not a bro-mance, obviously. But also unpleasant. I only wish it were something as simple as him preferring *The Sound of Music* to pinning and undercupping."

His eyes widened. "Hey, you know wrestling!"

"Older brother."

"So is he going to kick this cheating dude's ass?"

"Sam? No. He doesn't live here, and even if he did, there's absolutely no way I would tell him about this."

"How come?"

"Because he's a cop. And he's extremely overprotective." Though she didn't usually discuss it, for some reason, she found this guy very easy to talk to, so she added, "He sort of became my father when our parents died."

Ross leaned forward in his chair, dropping his elbows onto the table. His fingers brushed against her hand, in a move that was as fleeting as it was sweet. A faint brush of *I'm Sorry* and *How Sad* and *Hey, I Understand*. All unsaid. All understood.

All appreciated.

She cleared her throat, feeling the lump start to rise, the way it always did when this particular subject came up. "Anyway, I don't need Sam to fight my battles. I can take care of myself."

"I don't doubt it," Ross said.

"Don't worry, I'm really not the violent type. This guy didn't crush my spirit, he merely dinged my ego."

He held her stare, as if assessing the truth of her

words. Lucy stared right back, a tiny smile on her lips, relieved that she meant exactly what she'd said, hoping he realized that, too.

"I'm glad," he finally admitted, seeing the truth in her face.

"So am I."

"Still, if you change your mind and decide to get all saw-crazy on this boyfriend, remind me not to go with you. I wouldn't want to be arrested as an accomplice."

She chuckled as he turned her earlier words back on her, then clarified, "*Ex*-boyfriend." Shaking her head, she added, "Believe me, nothing could induce me to go back there." Then something occurred to her. "Oh, *no!*" Lucy put a hand over her forehead as she remembered something. Because she was going to have to make a liar of herself. "I'm so stupid!"

"What?"

"My brother's Christmas present to me. It came in the mail today—he sent it to Jude's place because he knows mail sometimes gets stolen from the building where I live and Jude's has a doorman." She felt moisture in her eyes, furious at herself for forgetting the gift, but also worried about what Jude would do with it. "He's probably already thrown it down the trash chute."

"Jude?" he said doubtfully. "Lemme guess—spoiled, rich punk?"

It might have taken a little while for the blinders to come off, but Lucy had to admit, that pretty well described her ex. "How'd you know?"

"Having a doorman in NYC is a pretty big tip-off. So's having a name like Jude. Plus, he must've done something pretty bad if you're fantasizing about chopping the head off his trouser snake, yet he'd still throw out a Christmas gift from your brother…meaning he's an immature, petulant brat." He spread his hands. "Or a spoiled, rich asshole."

"All of the above would cover it."

"And you're with this guy…why?"

"I'm not with him."

"But you were as of…"

She sighed deeply. "About two hours ago."

He whistled, leaning back in his chair, extending his long legs, crossed at the ankle. "Was it serious? I mean, were you guys exclusive?"

"Not according to him, apparently."

His jaw tightened a tiny bit. "And according to you?"

"Well, I thought so, but maybe I just saw things differently than he did. We'd been dating three months, but we hadn't even…you know. So maybe he cheated since he'd never gotten anywhere with me."

Ross coughed into his fist, apparently surprised she'd admitted that. Maybe he was turned-off; some guys would be at the thought that a girl would wait three months before getting down to business. If so, better to find out now if he was one of them.

Why that should be, she didn't know. After all, she might never even speak to this guy again once she left this shop. Somehow, the thought made her heart twist a lot harder than it had earlier when she'd thought about not seeing Jude anymore.

"Good for you," he said.

Okay, so he wasn't one of *those* guys, apparently. The realization warmed her a little on this very chilly day.

"Let him eat his heart out, wondering what he's thrown away."

She liked that idea. "I hope twenty years from now he's still wondering if he missed out on the best sex of his life."

Their stares locked as the heated words hung there between them. They were having a very intimate conversation for two strangers, and now, she suspected, they were both thinking a little too much about certain parts of that conversation

Like sex. Great sex. She might not have had it—great, or otherwise—but that didn't mean she was immune to desire. Looking at the man sitting across from her, feeling the heat sluice through her veins to settle with quiet, throbbing insistence between her thighs, she knew full well she had a basic understanding of want.

Or more than basic. Because it wasn't just her sex that was responding here. Every inch of her skin tingled as she thought of him touching her, pressing his mouth to all the more interesting parts of her body. Places that responded to the warm look in his eyes and how he opened his mouth to draw in a slow breath in a way they'd never responded to any guy's most passionate embrace.

His gaze dropped to her mouth and his voice was thick as he finally replied, "I almost feel sorry for the bastard."

She didn't. And she definitely didn't feel sorry for herself any longer. Not when, with one twenty-minute conversation, this complete stranger was introducing her to sensations her ex hadn't elicited in months of dating.

They remained silent for one more moment. Then, as if they both realized they were falling into something neither had anticipated—at the speed of light, no less—they shifted in their chairs and broke the stare.

Lucy forced a light laugh, trying to pretend she wasn't completely enraptured by the thought of pressing her mouth to the cord of muscle in his neck. "I'm not going to spare him any sympathy until I get my present back and make sure he didn't destroy it."

His gleaming eyes narrowed. "You really think he would?"

She considered it, remembered some of Jude's more spiteful moods. Not to mention his ridiculously misplaced indignation that she'd walked in on him today— as if it were all her fault because she'd caught him, not his that he'd cheated. "It's possible."

Ross's jaw clenched, a muscle flexing in his cheek. "Why don't you let me take care of this?"

"Why would you do that? You don't even know me."

"I know enough to know you shouldn't have to beg somebody who betrayed you to give you back something that's yours."

She heard the note of protectiveness in his voice, and found it strange. And very nice. Ross had just met her, yet he'd already been more thoughtful and considerate of her feelings than Jude had in the past three months.

"It's not that big a deal," she insisted, not wanting to drag somebody else into her troubles.

"It's from your only family member, Luce," he replied, shaking his head. "So of course it's a big deal. I want to make sure you get it back."

Lucy's breath caught. The soft way he'd said the nickname, Luce, seemed so tender. And the way he'd immediately understood why the gift from Sam was important to her, without her having to explain it…

Who are you? she couldn't help wondering. *Can you really be this nice a guy?*

"Do you think he'd really destroy your Christmas present?"

She didn't like to think so, but it was possible. "He was pretty mad when I left, mainly because I wouldn't stick around to listen to his explanation."

"Could there have been one?"

She snickered. "Sure." She tapped her finger on her cheek, as if thinking it over. "Hmm, okay, I have an idea how it could have, uh…*gone down.*"

A half smile lifted one corner of his oh-so-sexy mouth, as if he understood the reason for her inflection.

"So, his skanky neighbor was taking a bath, and she forgot she had no shampoo," Lucy explained. "Wrapped only in a towel, she came to his door to borrow some."

"Wait," he interrupted. "I bet I know what happened next. It just so happens, he was about to take a shower, too, so he was also only wearing a towel."

She giggled, wondering why she could already find this funny when it had brought tears to her eyes earlier today. More proof that her heart hadn't ever been involved in her relationship with Jude, she supposed.

"And then…hmm. Oh, I've got it," she said. "A pack of wild dogs somehow got into the building, rode up the elevator, burst into the apartment and ripped off both their towels. And in the ensuing struggle, slutty neighbor chick tripped and fell mouth first onto his sad, strange-looking little penis."

Ross winced. "Ouch."

"Ouch for her, or for him?"

"Well, mainly for you," he said, that gentle tone back in his voice. "For having to witness that." That sexy grin flashed. "But also ouch to him for having a sad, strange-looking little penis."

"Considering it was the first—and last—time I ever saw it, I can only say I'm glad I made the decision not to sleep with him."

"Me, too," he admitted, sounding as though he meant it. Which was odd, considering she didn't even know him and neither of them had any idea if they would ever share anything more than this one conversation at this one particular moment.

She hoped they would. It was fast, and utterly surprising and the timing was pretty bad. But she already had the feeling this sexy, hardworking guy was someone special. And even if the timing was all wrong, she might be the one with lifelong regrets if she didn't at least give this more time to play out.

"So, do you always go around telling strangers about your sex life?" he asked.

She played with her coffee cup, tracing her fingers on its rim, not meeting his eyes. "You're the first," she admitted. Hoping she wouldn't reveal too much, she shrugged and added, "You just don't seem like a stranger."

He didn't. She felt like she was already starting to know him, or at least know the essence of him. The physical attraction had been instant. But there was so much more. Earlier, when she'd mentioned her parents, there'd been that warmth, the smile, the tender looks, that ever-so-gentle brush of his fingers against her hand. Then there was his reaction to her having been cheated on. His indignation over her lost Christmas present.

All those things told a story. A nice one. A good one.

A story she wanted to explore a little more. Or a lot more.

"Okay then, if we're not strangers, I guess that means we're friends," he told her with a tender smile. Then, without explanation, he pushed the chair back and stood up. She wasn't sure what he intended—to leave, to ask her out?—until he extended a hand to her.

"So, come on, friend. Let's go reclaim your Christmas present."

CONSIDERING HOW BEAUTIFUL Lucy was, Ross didn't expect her ex to be a total dog, even if he was a total dick. There had to have been something she'd found attractive about the guy. And even though he hadn't known her long, he already felt pretty sure it hadn't been the money. She just didn't seem the type. There wasn't a fake thing about her…and he should know. He'd looked. Hard.

Hell, it had been impossible *not* to look, not to try to get to know everything about her. Sitting across from each other at that coffee shop, they'd fallen into an easy, laid-back conversation that it had taken him a half-dozen meetings to achieve with other girls. Then things had gone from warm and friendly to hot and expectant.

He shouldn't have started thinking about Lucy's sex life, much less talking about it. Because it was damned hard to get it out of his mind—or to stop wondering about that look she'd had in her eye during the long silence they'd shared.

Walking outside to drop off his tools in his truck, then to the subway so they could ride up to her dopey ex's neighborhood, he found himself more surprised by her with every move she made.

She never stopped talking, but didn't jabber about stupid, inane stuff. He didn't once hear the word shoes. Or makeup. Or shopping.

She talked about the city—how much she loved the energy of it, the pace, the excitement.

She stopped to take pictures—things that would never occur to him to be interesting, like a pile of trash bags or an old rusty bike against a fence.

She talked about her plans to go to Europe after she graduated, to photograph anything that moved and lots of things that didn't.

She bought one of those disgusting hot dogs off a cart, and actually ate the thing.

She passed a five dollar bill to a homeless guy. She also dropped another five into a bell-ringer's bucket, even as she admitted she didn't really like Christmas, claiming her favorite response to anyone's "Merry Christmas," was "Bah, humbug!"

He had a hard time buying that one. She was too cute and sweet and generous to be a Scrooge. But he did see the shadow in her expression whenever she talked about the holiday and suspected she was serious about disliking it.

Other than that, though, she laughed a lot. She smiled at strangers. She turned her face up to meet the softly falling snow and licked its moisture off her lips. Sweet laugh, beautiful smile, sexy lips.

All in all, aside from totally attracting him, she charmed him. It was an old-fashioned description, but it fit. Lucy was, quite simply, charming. Plus adorable. And hot as hell. Every minute he spent with her made him like her even more…and made him more determined to ensure her cheating ex didn't get the chance to hurt her again.

She was, in short, fantastic. So, no, he definitely didn't see her hooking up with someone who had no redeeming qualities whatsoever. This Jude guy, who lived in a high-rise building with apartments that probably cost five times the rent in his own tiny place, had to have something to attract someone like Lucy.

Then he met the loser, face-to-face, and understood.

Jude Zacharias was spoiled, handsome and smooth—one of those old-money types whose family name probably hadn't been tainted by the stench of real work for a few generations. But the main thing about him, the thing that would suck in any girl, was the earnest charm.

He laid it on thick from the minute he answered the door and saw Lucy. He even managed to work up a couple of tears in his eyes as he told her how sorry he was that he'd let some skank trick him into doing something bad—*ha*—how much he wished he could take it back and how glad he was that she'd returned.

Then he spotted Ross, who'd been hovering just out of sight, near the hallway wall.

"Who the fuck is *he?*"

Stepping forward, Ross said, "He the fuck is Lucy's friend, Ross. We're here to pick up the package she left behind. Now, would you get it, please? We're in a hurry."

Yeah. Not because he had errands to run, but because he was in a rush to get Lucy away from this prick who'd hurt her, even if it had been her pride, not her heart that had been dinged. Honestly, he'd wanted to rip the guy's hand off when he'd actually reached out and tried to touch her. Fortunately, Lucy had stepped aside, out of reach.

The guy's jaw hit his chest. He gaped, then sputtered, finally saying, "Who *are* you?"

Ross looked at Lucy and shrugged. "Is he brain damaged or something? Like I said, I'm Ross. I'm here to make sure you give Lucy her package, and that you don't try anything."

"Lucy, are you serious? Did you bring this guy to throw in my face, make me jealous or something?" He reached for her hand. "Babe, you don't have to do that, you know I'll take you back."

"Dude, get over it. You've been dumped," Ross said.

Jude's glare would have fried an egg. "Mind your own damn business. Why the hell are you here anyway?"

Lucy stepped between them. "Ross is a friend."

"Yeah, sure, right. How long has he been your... *friend?*"

She tapped a finger on her lips, as if thinking about it, then cast a quick, mischievous glance toward Ross. "Oh, about an hour now."

Jude sputtered. Lucy ignored him.

"He just wanted to come along in case you decided to be a jerk about my package."

The guy sneered. "Oh, yeah? And what's he gonna do if I say you can't have it?"

Ross's fingers curled into fists and his jaw tightened. He took a step toward the door. He couldn't remember if he'd ever felt this anxious to punch someone but he didn't think so. Something about hearing the way this little asshole talked to Lucy brought out the overprotective he-man in him.

She put up a hand, stopping him. "It's okay. Jude, please don't be a pain about this. Can I just have my package?" She reached into her purse and pulled out a key ring. "And here, you should have this back."

He snatched the key out of her hand, cast one more glare at Ross, then stepped back into the apartment. He returned a few seconds later, shoving a small, paper-wrapped carton toward her. It was mashed, dirty, slightly torn.

Lucy stared at it, her bottom lip trembling, then took it. A small shake elicited a tinkling sound from inside. The paper in which it was wrapped was damp.

Whatever had been inside had contained some kind of liquid. And it was broken.

"You didn't," she whispered, her voice thick. Her eyes were wet with unshed tears.

Jude shrugged. "Hey, just figured it must not have been important if you left it here, so I was gonna pitch it."

It looked as though the bastard already had. Against a wall.

Furious, Ross took another step toward him. "You petty little douchebag." This time, Lucy was too distracted by the ruined gift in her hands to stop him.

Good. That left Ross free to grab a fistful of her ex-boyfriend's top and shove him back into his apartment. The guy tripped over a table, stumbling backward a few steps before falling on his arrogant ass.

"Take another step and I'll call the cops!" he shrieked. Obviously pretty boy wasn't used to anybody threatening his perfect, spoiled little self.

"I could knock out your teeth before they get here," Ross growled.

The other guy scrambled backward as Ross stalked him, step by step.

"Look, I'm sorry, okay?" he said. "Lucy, come on, you know I wouldn't do anything to hurt you. It was an accident."

"Accident my ass," Ross said as he leaned down and hauled the guy up by the collar of his J. Crew sweater.

His right hand curled into a fist but before he could let it fly, Lucy grabbed his arm. "Let him go. Please, Ross, let's just get out of here." She cast her ex a withering look. "Hey, he did me a favor. If there was any doubt in my mind that he's a disgusting, hateful person, this eliminated it."

"Babe…"

"Bite me, Jude," she snapped.

Ross grinned, then, for good measure, pushed the dude backward until he hit the couch, sprawling out on it.

Ross glanced at Lucy, seeing she'd hugged the package to her chest, apparently not caring that it was wet. It was like seeing someone who'd lost their most prized possession. Nobody deserved to be cheated on, humiliated and then, to top it all off, have something important to them shattered. Remembering what she'd said about it being just the two of them after their parents had died, he felt his heart twist in his chest, knowing how much her brother's gift must have meant to her.

His own family drove him crazy sometimes—especially his overly controlling father—but he couldn't imagine life without them. She was so young to bear that kind of sadness. One thing he knew, Lucy Fleming had to be one hell of a strong young woman. And a forgiving one, if she was determined to stop him from kicking her ex's ass.

"Please, can we just go?" she asked.

Yeah. She seemed pretty determined. That was lucky for the ex, even though it didn't make Ross too happy.

"Fine," he told her.

He took her arm and led her to the door, glancing back over his shoulder before they walked through it. The ex still sat there on the couch, a sneer curling his lips. As if he were the injured party in this whole rotten mess.

The boiling well of anger inside him had rolled back to a slow simmer, and Ross knew he had to get out of here before it boiled back up. Mr. J. Crew dickhead had finally realized the merits of shutting the hell up, but that look on his face was seriously pissing Ross off. If he opened his mouth again, or if one single tear fell out of Lucy's eyes, he was gonna go postal on the squirmy punk.

Her hand tightened on his arm, as if she knew what he was thinking. So he wouldn't do it. But something wouldn't let him leave without one more parting shot. "Hey, dude, don't worry, I wouldn'ta hit you. Wouldn't risk damaging that pretty face of yours, 'cause it sounds to me like you really need it."

"What do you mean?" the other man snapped, starting to rise from his seat. Emboldened, perhaps, by the thought that Ross was admitting he wouldn't have hit him?

Just give me a reason, punk.

Ross shrugged as Lucy stepped into the hallway ahead of him. "I mean, it sounds like you need whatever help you can get. From what I hear, you not only have a scrawny neck, you have a scrawny dick as well." *Tsking,* he shook his head. "Even worse, a sad, strange-looking one."

The other guy's face erupted in scarlet, and he sputtered, but couldn't come up with anything to say. Which, in Ross's mind, confirmed what Lucy had said about him. A guy with an ounce of self-confidence would have laughed, or sneered. Jude just looked like he wanted to call Mommy and make the new kid stop saying mean things to him.

"Oh, by the way," he added. "Happy birthday."

Ross slammed the door, not waiting for Jude to come up with a crushing reply. Not that he could, really, because, man, any guy who couldn't defend himself against small-cock accusations didn't have much of a leg to stand on.

It wasn't until they were alone in the elevator, heading toward the bottom floor, that he looked down and saw Lucy's shoulders shaking. It was as if she'd held herself together, keeping her emotions in check until she got out of sight of her ex, but now that they were alone, her sadness over the day's events had come crashing down on her.

He turned her toward him. Ross fully intended to take her into his arms, awkwardly pat her back or whatever guys did to console crying women. But before he could do it, he realized he'd made a big mistake.

"Oh…my…God…" she said between gasps, which weren't caused by tears, but rather, by laughter. She looked up at him, her lips shaking, her eyes twinkling with merriment. "Did you see his face?"

"I saw," he said, smiling down at her, so pleased she

wasn't brokenhearted over creepy Jude that he wanted to pick her up and swing her around in his arms.

"Thank you so much," she said. "You were my knight in shining armor."

He grinned and gestured toward his bomber jacket. "Carpenter in tarnished leather, at best."

Her pretty mouth widened in a smile. "Either way... my hero." Then, still looking playful, happy, appreciative, she rose on her tiptoes and reached up to brush her delicate fingers against his cheek. He had about a second to process what she was about to do before she pressed her soft lips against his.

It was a thank-you kiss, he had no doubt about that.

Sweet. Tender. Simple.

Incredibly good.

It should have been nothing but a three-second brush of skin on skin, an expression of gratitude between two people who didn't really know each other yet but definitely wanted to.

But damned if Ross was willing to let it go down that way. Once he felt Lucy's mouth, shared her sweet breath, impulse took over. He lifted both hands, cupping one around her cheek. The other he tangled in her long, thick hair, taking pure pleasure in the softness of it, letting it glide through his fingers like water.

He deepened the kiss, sliding his tongue out to tease hers. Lucy groaned slightly, taking what he offered and upping the ante even more by tilting her head and widening her mouth. *Thank you* and *you're welcome* turned into *I-want-you* and *where's the nearest bed* in about ten seconds flat. Sweetness faded and heat erupted as their tongues thrust and twined.

"Ahem."

It took a second for the voice to intrude. But another throat-clearing and a titter finally invaded his Lucy-infused consciousness. It appeared they'd arrived at the bottom floor. The door had slid open and they were providing quite a show for the people waiting in the lobby.

Filled with regret, he pulled away, looking down into her pretty, flushed face, seeing the way her long lashes rested on her high cheekbones. She kept her eyes closed a moment longer, swaying a little toward him. But the box pressed against her chest prevented her from melting into his body.

And their sudden, unwelcome audience prevented him from moving the box.

"We're here," he whispered.

Her eyes flew open. Seeing the strangers watching them—two young men with their arms around each other's waists, both grinning widely, and an older, white-haired woman whose grin was, if possible, even wider—Lucy stammered an apology.

"No need to apologize," one of the men said, waving his hand as Lucy and Ross exited the elevator.

The other nodded in agreement. "Tell me this means you ditched 6C."

Lucy's jaw fell open. "Wha…?"

"He's a bad egg," the woman said, jumping into the conversation as if they had all known each other for years. In truth, Ross suspected they were complete strangers to Lucy. "A total fart-weasel."

Ross coughed into his fist at the description, but the two men were already nodding in agreement. "He sure is."

"Have we met?" Lucy asked, shaking her head in confusion, confirming Ross's suspicion.

"No," said the darker-haired man. "But we all live

on six, too. And honey, 6C is just *nasty*. So not your type!"

"Thanks," she murmured, looking even more embarrassed than before. Considering complete strangers were dissecting her love life, he could see why.

The light-haired man eyed Ross. "Did you beat him up?"

"No."

Ms. Elderly Busybody sighed heavily. "That's too bad. I've been hoping somebody would. That boy could benefit from an ass-whupping."

"Well, given what I know of him so far, I have no doubt that someday your prayers will be answered," Ross said.

He and Lucy murmured goodbyes to their three new friends, then headed for the door. As they approached him, the doorman offered Lucy a conspiratorial wink, as if he agreed with the other residents' opinion of her ex. Which was nice, but probably had to be making Lucy feel even worse about ever having dated the fart-weasel in 6C.

He reached for her hand and squeezed it. "Don't beat yourself up about it."

She sucked in a surprised breath, and stopped half-way across the lobby. Looking up at him, she appeared shocked that he'd been able to figure out what she'd been thinking.

"He's a con artist, Luce," Ross said with a simple shrug. "He became what you wanted him to be."

"Yes, he did," she murmured. "But how did you know?"

"Guys do it all the time, especially with girls who

won't, uh…." He didn't want to be crass enough to say *put out,* though that was what he meant.

"Gotcha," she said. "And thanks for not telling me I was a complete idiot for not seeing it sooner."

"You *did* see it," he told her, not liking that self-recrimination in her voice. "Which is probably why you wouldn't, uh…"

This time, during the pregnant pause while they both mentally filled in the blank, Lucy actually laughed. "You really are a nice guy, aren't you?"

"I have a few ex-girlfriends who would disagree, but my parents like to think so."

"I think I'll have to side with your folks on that one."

"I'll be sure to tell them that," he said with a grin.

She grinned back, then, without another word, slipped her hand into his and turned again toward the exit.

As her soft fingers entwined with his, Ross's heart jolted. He'd kissed her, touched her…but this was a little bit more. It wasn't just a simple touch. That clasped hand was so easy and relaxed, like she already trusted him, as if they'd known each other for weeks rather than hours.

He honestly wasn't sure what was going to happen when they walked out of this building. He'd done what he'd set out to do—escorted her to her ex's place to retrieve her present. But now what? They'd made no other plans. It was the day before Christmas Eve, the streets were a madhouse, he had a million things to do. But as they walked into the bracing December day, alive with the thrum of city life, laughter, and energy, all he could think was that the very last thing he wanted was to say goodbye to her.

5

Now
Chicago, December 23, 2011

THOUGH HE KNEW STELLA had the checks for the subcontractors ready, Ross was hoping it would take a while for her to find Lucy's. While there were still people in the building, it would be far too easy for her to slip away. The longer it took, the better the chances were that she wouldn't be able to avoid him on her way out.

Yet somehow, she nearly pulled it off. He didn't even realize she was leaving until he spotted a thick head of dark hair—topped by a merry green, feathered elf cap—getting onto the elevator. "Damn it," he muttered.

"What?"

Seeing the surprised expression on the face of one of his project managers, who'd stopped to chat after Mr. Whitaker departed, Ross mumbled, "I'm sorry, I just remembered something I forgot to take care of."

Like getting Lucy's address, phone number and her promise to get together very soon so they could talk. Exactly what they'd talk about, he didn't know. Six years seemed like a long time for a how've-you-been type of conversation. So maybe they'd skip how've-you-beens in favor of what-happens-now?

Then he remembered that Stella had hired Lucy. She had to know how to get in touch with her. Plus, Lucy had mentioned she lived here, worked here—it shouldn't be hard to find her online.

So, yes, he could be reasonable and mature and patient about this. Could wait until after the holidays, then call her sometime in January to say hello and see if she'd like to meet.

But something—maybe the look in her eyes when she'd said he would know what she'd been up to if he'd called during the past six years—wouldn't let him wait. He couldn't have said it in front of anyone at the party; wasn't sure he'd have found the words even if they'd been left alone. Still, Lucy deserved an explanation from him. Even if she thought it a lame one and decided to keep hating him, he'd feel better if he offered it.

Then he'd get to work on making her not hate him anymore.

"Thanks for the party, Mr. Marshall," his employee said. "The kids really loved it."

"I'm glad. Hey, you and your family have a great holiday," Ross replied, already stepping toward the enclosed stairs that were intended for emergencies.

This was one. The elevator could have made a few stops on the way to the lobby—there were still employees on other floors, closing down for the holiday break. If he hustled, he might beat her to the bottom.

He might not be slinging a hammer and doing hard physical labor ten hours a day anymore, but Ross did keep himself busy in his off hours. So the dash down six flights of stairs didn't really wind him. By the time he burst through the doors into the tiled lobby of the building—surprising Chip, the elderly security guard—the elevator door was just sliding open, and several people exited, some carrying boxes, bags of gifts, plates of food, files to work on at home.

One carried nothing, but wore a silly hat.

Lucy saw him and her mouth dropped. "How did you…?"

"Staircase," he told her. "Were you really going to leave without saying goodbye?"

"Did you really stalk me down six flights of stairs?"

He rolled his eyes. "Stalking? That's a little dramatic."

"You're breathing hard and sweating," she accused him, stepping close and frowning. "Don't even try to tell me you didn't run every step of the way."

He couldn't contain a small grin. "Busted."

"The question is, why?"

"Here's a better one. Why'd you leave without saying goodbye?"

"We said our goodbyes a long time ago," she retorted.

He whistled.

"What?"

"You're still really mad at me."

Those slim shoulders straightened and her chin went up. "That's ridiculous."

Lucy was obviously trying for a withering look, but with that silly hat and the droopy feather hanging by her cheek, she only managed freaking adorable. He couldn't resist lifting a hand and nudging the feather back into place, his fingertips brushing against the soft skin of her cheek.

She flinched as if touched with a hot iron. "Don't."

"Jesus, Lucy, do you hate me?" he whispered, realizing for the first time that this might not be mere bravado. Was it possible that over the past six years, while he'd been feeling miserable even as he congratulated himself on doing the right—the mature—thing, she'd been hating his guts?

"Of course I don't hate you," she said, sounding huffy. As if she was telling the truth, but wasn't exactly happy about that fact.

So she *wanted* to hate him?

"Can we please go sit down somewhere and have a cup of coffee?"

A wistful expression crossed her face, as if she, too, were remembering their first meeting in that New York coffee shop.

"I can't," she murmured. "I need to get to the bank before it closes, and before the snow starts."

"I'll walk with you."

"I'm driving."

"I'll ride with you."

She huffed. "You're still persistent, aren't you?"

"Only when it's important."

"And when did I become important to you?"

The day we met. He didn't say the words, but he suspected she saw them in his face.

"Look, Ross, I swear, I am not holding a grudge," she said. "So you don't have to go out of your way to try to make up with me."

"That's not what I'm doing. I just…I've missed you. A lot."

"How can you miss someone you knew for only a weekend, years ago?"

"Are you telling me you don't feel the same way?"

If she said she didn't, he'd make himself believe her. He'd let her go. Chalk this up to one of those life lessons where a memory of a time you'd considered perfect turned out to be something less than that to the one you'd shared it with.

Lucy didn't respond at first. Not wanting her to breeze over this, to reply without thought, Ross lifted a hand. A few strands of her silky, dark hair had fallen against her face. He slid his fingers through it, sending heat all the way up his arm. Her eyes drifted closed, the long lashes stark against her pale skin. And he'd swear she curled her face into his hand for an instant.

Ross groaned, as helpless to resist her now as he'd been that first day, in the elevator. Ignoring the surprised stare of the guard, who was the only other person in the lobby, he bent to Lucy and brushed his lips against hers, softly, demanding nothing more than a chance.

She hesitated for the briefest moment, then melted against him. This time there was no crumpled box separating their bodies; he was thrilled to discover she still fit against him as perfectly as ever. Her soft curves welcomed his harder angles, her feet parting a little as she brushed her legs against his and arched into him.

Sweetness flared into desire, just like it had the first time they'd kissed. Ross dropped his hands to her hips and held her close. Sweeping his tongue into her mouth, he dared her to go further. She, of course, took the dare, accepting what he offered and upping the ante by lifting her arms to encircle his neck. Their tongues thrust together, hot and languorous and deep, leaving Ross to wonder how he'd ever even imagined kissing any other woman had been as good as kissing this one. Everything about her was as intoxicating to him as it had been then. Maybe more so—because Lucy was no longer the sweet-faced co-ed. She was now every inch a woman. And he'd had the intense privilege of making her that woman.

Maybe that's what made this kiss different from their first one. Then, there'd been curiosity and wonder, riding on a wave of pure attraction.

Now they knew what they could be to each other. Knew the pleasure they were capable of creating together. Knew what it was like to be naked and hot and joined together as sanity retreated and hunger took over every waking thought. And many sleeping ones.

She lifted her leg slightly, twining it around his, and Ross echoed the tiny groan she made when she arched harder against him. There was no way she couldn't feel his rock-hard erection, any more than he could miss the heat between the thighs that instinctively cradled him.

Six years fell away, along with time, place and any concerns about an audience. There was just this, just the two of them, exploring something that had been missing from their lives for far too long.

Though he felt lost to everything else in the world except Lucy, Ross did finally become aware of a throat-clearing—Chip?—followed by a dinging sound that indicated the arrival of the elevator. A *swoosh* of the door was followed by a dull roar of laughing voices; the last few partiers…i.e., his employers, were about to make their way home.

He and Lucy quickly ended the kiss and stepped

apart. "Déjà vu all over again," he muttered. Only this time, they'd been caught on the *outside* of the elevator.

She actually laughed a little, that sweet, warm laugh that was so distinctly hers. Over the past several years, he'd listened for that sound, always expecting to somehow hear it again, even though he'd never really let himself believe he would.

"Hopefully we're not going to hear some old lady say the guy on six is a fart-weasel."

"Hey, my office is on six," he said with a chuckle, pleased to realize Lucy remembered as much about that day as he did.

A group exited the elevator. "Have a happy holiday!" said one of his workers, who walked with his pregnant wife.

Ross nodded at the couple, and at the three others who'd come down with them. "Same to you. Be careful out there—it's supposed to be a bad one."

Murmuring their goodbyes, the group headed for the exit. They were escorted by Chip, who turned a key to operate the intricate, electronic locks that turned this place into a fortress. With the offices closed to the public today, Chip had been kept on his toes playing doorman, letting employees in for the party, and, now that it was over, back out.

Fortunately the guard never complained. Not even about the fact that he had to work all night, during an impending blizzard, right before Christmas Eve. They might not have state secrets to be stolen, but some of their competitors would risk a lot for the chance to get at prebid documents. With millions of dollars in high-end construction projects at stake, corporate espionage had never been more of a danger. Plus, Elite had invested a hell of a lot of money in computers and equipment. Keeping security on-site 24/7 was one place where Ross had stood firm against his penny-pinching father, who loved to keep a hand in the business even though he was technically retired.

"Wait, I'm leaving, too," Lucy said as Chip began to relock the doors.

"Lucy…"

She held up a hand and brushed past him. "Please, Ross, I really need to go."

Hell, she sounded more determined to leave than she had before he'd kissed her. Not that he regretted it. Not one bit.

Chip glanced toward Ross, as if asking what Ross wanted him to do. He nodded once. He couldn't keep Lucy here against her will. Nothing had changed; he'd taken his shot, and he'd lost.

But just for now.

Definitely. They'd been caught off guard, taken completely by surprise when they'd bumped into one another today. Now, though, he knew Lucy was living in Chicago. There was no longer any geographic reason for him to bow out. Nor was he young enough—angry and resentful enough—to let outside situations and demands make him walk away from her for a second time.

It was as if she'd been delivered back into his life, like the best kind of Christmas gift. The one you never expected, didn't realize you needed, but, when you tore off the paper, suddenly understood that it was exactly what you'd been waiting for.

No, he wasn't about to let her get away again, but he knew the old saying about picking your battles. Lucy had her guard up, she was uncomfortable here on his turf and hadn't had a moment to evaluate what all this meant to her. So he'd give her a few days to figure things out, then try again. And the next time he asked her to hear him out, he would not take no for an answer.

"Goodbye, Ross," she said, not even turning around to face him. Her voice was soft, low, and he suspected she was trying desperately not to reveal her emotions.

He had to let her go. Had to trust that was the right thing to do in order to get her back.

"Goodbye," he replied. "And Lucy?"

She hesitated, then glanced back at him over her shoulder.

"Merry Christmas."

A brief hesitation, then a tiny smile widened her perfect lips. "Bah humbug."

And then she disappeared out into the gray twilight.

It usually took twenty minutes to get to the nearest branch of her bank. But today, Lucy was dealing with Friday evening, holiday weekend, impending-blizzard traffic. So she didn't reach the drive-thru until right before they closed at seven.

Thick flecks of white started to appear on the windshield of her Jeep as she waited in the long line of cars. New York got the white stuff by the foot, but here, the Snow Miser seemed to delight in sending wicked, bone-chilling winds along with his icy droppings. The flakes weren't the sweet, delicate ones that gently kissed your bare face. These were big, sloppy and wet, landing like punches, instead.

Once she'd made her deposit, Lucy headed right home. Luckily she had believed the weatherman's warnings and gone shopping yesterday. Having stocked up on chocolate, Diet Coke, and DVDs, she looked forward to a weekend inside, chomping on junk food, watching disaster movies, and shopping online.

Her trip home was difficult, even though the Jeep had 4-wheel drive. Her main concern was seeing through the swirling blanket of white in front of the windshield. Chicago was usually a bright city, even at night; yet this kind of snowstorm didn't reflect the light the way some did. It instead sucked it in, making streetlights hard to see.

It took almost two hours. By the time she arrived at her apartment building, she was not only cold and tired, she was actually jumpy from having been so on-alert.

Once inside her place, she wrenched off her coat and headed for the bathroom. A hot bath sounded like the perfect way to de-stress. She promised herself that, once in that bath, she would not spend one minute thinking about Ross. Or about that kiss.

Why did you have to go and kiss him back?

Probably because she'd been curious, wondering if her memories had been faulty. Could their brief relationship really have been as intense as she'd told herself it was? Had every other man she'd been with really paled in comparison, or was it wishful imaginings of the one that got away?

That kiss had answered all her questions: she hadn't imagined a damn thing.

"Stop thinking about it," she ordered herself as she got into the tub. The hot water stung her skin at first, but she welcomed the sensation, welcomed anything that would take her mind off the man she'd been kissing just a couple of hours ago.

It didn't work. Ross became more prominent in her thoughts. Not just the Ross of today, but the one she'd known before. The guy with whom she'd been so incredibly intimate.

The warmth, the fragrance of the bubble bath, the darkness of the room, lit only with candlelight—all seduced her. The sensation of water hitting every inch of her—between her thighs, caressing the tips of her breasts—made all her nerve endings leap up to attention.

But when it came to really turning her on, her brain did the heavy lifting. It was too easy to remember the magical feel of his hands on her body, the sweet, sexy way he kissed, the groans of pleasure he made when he came.

Her hand slid down, scraping across her slick skin, teasing the puckered tip of one breast. The contact sent warmth spiraling downward, until her sex throbbed. Her eyes closed, her head back, it was easy to think *his* hands were on her, *his* fingers delicately stroking her clit until she began to sigh.

She gave herself over to desire, and let her mind float free. Memories gave way to imagination and her body, starved of physical connection for many months—since she'd left New York—reacted appropriately. Before too long, a slow, warm orgasm slid through her. She sighed a little, quivering and savoring it. But the deliciousness went away far too quickly.

It just couldn't compare to the real thing. To Lucy, getting off had never been the point; it had been sharing the experience that she loved. And she couldn't deny it, even after all these years, after the silence and the regret, she wanted to share that experience with him.

She quickly finished her bath, replaying the day's events as she washed her hair. As she thought everything over, including the way she'd tried to skulk out of the building when his back was turned, something started to nag at the back of her brain. She couldn't put her finger on it at first, just feeling like there was something she had forgotten. Something important.

It wasn't until she was dressed in a comfortable pair of sweats, with her hair wrapped in a towel, that she realized what it was. "Oh, no!" she yelped.

Lucy ran to the living room of her apartment, seeing her purse on the table. Alone. "You *idiot!*"

Because, though she hoped and prayed she'd just forgotten to bring it in from her Jeep, she seriously feared she'd left her most precious possessions at the Elite Construction office: her camera bag and her very expensive specialty lenses.

She perched on a chair, trying to picture every moment. She remembered putting her equipment down on Santa's seat before leaving with Stella. When she'd returned, she'd seen Ross. Desperate to get away without being seen, she'd hurried onto the elevator. Without stopping to grab her camera bag and lens case.

"Damn it," she snapped, trying to decide if this was just bad or catastrophic. She had some big jobs lined up next week. Monday's was with a very wealthy family, who wanted to sit for a holiday portrait at their home. They were the kind of people who could really give her a leg up with the Magnificent Mile set.

Unfortunately Lucy remembered what Stella had

said about the Elite office: after tonight, they'd be shutting down until January.

She glanced at the clock—almost ten. Then out the window. The snow still fell steadily, but it appeared the wind had died down some. She could actually see down to the parking lot, could make out cars slowly driving by on the main street, which had been plowed, though the lot itself hadn't been.

If the office was downtown, or as far away as the bank, she probably wouldn't risk it. But it was close, maybe two miles. And the security guard could still be working. There was no guarantee that would be the case on Monday, especially if the whole city was snowed in until then.

Of course, if that happened, her own portrait appointment could be canceled as well. But if it weren't— if the weatherman had overestimated this time, and everything was fine Monday—did she really want to risk not having the equipment she needed to do the job?

Convinced, Lucy raced to her room and changed into jeans and a thick sweater. Adding boots and her warmest coat, she headed outside. The snow on her car was heavy and wet, and every minute she spent clearing it reminded her she was crazy to go chasing after a camera at the start of a blizzard.

Fortunately, as soon as she exited the parking lot and got onto the slushy road, she could tell things were better than when she'd come home an hour ago. The snow was heavier, yes, but she didn't have to crane forward and press her nose against the windshield to see out. It appeared old man winter was giving her a break—a short, wind-free window. She only hoped it didn't slam shut until after she got back home.

The drive that had taken her a few minutes this morning took her fifteen tonight. But when she reached the parking lot for Elite Construction and saw the security vehicle parked there, plus the warm, welcoming lights on the first floor, she was glad she'd taken the chance.

Parking, she hurried to the entrance and pounded on the door. The man inside was so startled, he nearly fell off his stool. He came closer, calling, "We're closed!"

"I know," she said, then pulled her hood back so he could see her face. Hopefully he'd remember her, if for no other reason than that she'd been making out with one of his coworkers a few hours ago. "Remember me? I was here earlier."

He nodded and smiled. Pulling out a large key ring, he unlocked the door, and ushered her in. "Goodness, miss, what are you doing out on a night like this?"

"I wouldn't be if I weren't desperate." She stomped her feet on a large mat. "I need to get upstairs to where the party was held. I forgot something and I have to get it tonight."

"Must be pretty important," he said, his gray eyebrows coming together. "It's not a fit night out for man nor beast."

She chuckled, recognizing the quote from a show she'd loved as a kid. "Do you think you could let me go look for my things?"

"I'll take you up. Gotta make my rounds, anyway."

He escorted her to the bank of elevators, and punched in a number on a keypad by the nearest one. The light above it came on, and the door slid open. Pretty high-tech stuff. Of course, she'd noticed earlier today that the new building had all the latest bells and whistles.

Arriving on the sixth floor, Lucy hurried to the area where the photo booth had been set up. It had been dismantled. Santa's chair was gone, and so were her bag and case. "Oh, hell."

"Some stuff was left in the break room," he told her. "If it's valuable, it's possible somebody locked it up for you."

"Could be. Stella saw me leave my camera and lenses here."

"Let's check her office first, then," he said, leading her down the hallway to the executive suite. He preceded her inside, but before she even had a chance to follow, she heard him exclaim, "Oh, no, watch it, mister!"

Following his stare, she looked out the window to the street below, and saw a car spinning out of control. It skidded off the street, hydroplaning across the parking lot where the Elite Construction security truck was parked. She winced, doubting the driver could regain control.

He didn't.

"Dang it all," said the guard. He cast her a quick look. "Do you mind looking by yourself? I should run down and make sure that driver's all right. If your stuff's not here, check the break room, back down the hall, fourth door on the left."

"Of course," she said, then watched the elderly man hurry away. She quickly scanned the office area. No luck. She wasn't going to go snooping through Stella's desk drawers or file cabinet, even if they weren't locked. Her things wouldn't fit, anyway.

She next spent several minutes searching the break room. It was piled with boxes of decorations, and containers of unopened food. Lucy looked through every bag and box, to be sure nobody had tucked her things in there for safekeeping.

Growing frustrated—and worrying somebody might have picked up the camera and lenses and given themselves an early Christmas present—she opened a freestanding cabinet and at last, struck pay dirt. "Yes!" she exclaimed, spying the familiar bag and case.

So relieved she felt like crying, she scooped them up, hurried toward the elevator and pushed the call button. She waited. And waited. And waited. Nothing.

Apparently the guard needed to again enter the code on the keypad so she could get down. Wondering if he could still be outside after all this time, she went to the front window and looked down toward the parking lot.

What she saw surprised her. An ambulance, its lights flashing, was parked beside the two vehicles involved in the fender-bender. She hadn't realized the crash had been so serious, but apparently the driver had been hurt. They were putting him on a gurney and wheeling him over to the ambulance.

Suddenly that gurney was pushed under a streetlight, and she had a better view of the person on it. Even through the snow and the darkness she could make out the grizzled gray hair, not to mention the uniform.

It wasn't the driver of the other car. It was the guard.

"Oh, God!" she muttered, wondering what had happened.

He'd gone out to help the accident victim—had he slipped and fallen? Or, maybe he'd been trying to help dig the vehicle out of a snowbank. Considering his age, and knowing even the healthiest of men could be affected when they tried to shovel too-heavy snow, she prayed he hadn't had a heart attack.

Then she began to wonder something else.

What if she was trapped in this building?

Her heart started thudding as she replayed everything in her mind. The conscientious way the man had carefully locked the door this afternoon, even though people were still leaving. And the way he'd obviously kept the elevator turned off tonight, despite knowing she was up here.

Would he really… "No," she muttered, certain he wouldn't have locked her in when he went to help the other driver.

There was only one way to be sure. Remembering how Ross had beat her to the lobby today, she found a door marked Stairs and headed through it. Six flights down was not fun, but it was better than sitting in somebody's office all night.

Reaching the entrance, she held her breath and pushed the nearest door. It didn't budge. Neither did the one beside it, or the next. She really was locked in here.

"Every building has an emergency exit," she reminded herself. She just had to find it. How difficult could that be?

Not difficult at all.

At least, she didn't think so…until the power went out.

6

Then
New York, December 23, 2005

AS THEY WALKED THE BUSY streets of the city, Ross
glanced at his watch and saw it was almost four o'clock.
He began to do some mental calculations. What time
did the shipping place close? How many people were
lined up there already? How long would it take to get
back to his place and pick up the wrapped presents?

Eventually he just started to wonder how much
money he had in his checking account. He needed to
know that, since he suspected he wasn't going to make
it to the mailing store today to send off gifts to his
family. He had lost track of time with Lucy; plus, he
hadn't even picked up something for his nephew yet.
So it looked like he'd be paying a king's ransom to send
it tomorrow and arrange for a Christmas Day delivery.
If there was such a thing.

For some reason, though, that didn't bother him as
much as he'd have expected. It seemed worth the price
since it had let him spend more time with Lucy Flem-

ing. After the unpleasant scene with her ex, followed by that amazing kiss in the elevator, he hadn't been about to say *nice meeting you* and walk away. Errands could wait. Plus, if worse came to worst, he could always send the family e-gift cards tomorrow. Having twenty-five bucks to spend at Amazon would make even his bratty youngest sister squeal; she was really into those teen romance books.

With a fallback plan in place, he let himself forget about everything else—missing the holidays with his family for the first time in his life. The job he was starting next week. The tense phone call he'd had with his father last week. It was sure to be repeated on Christmas Day, when talk would shift from turkey and Mom's great stuffing to the same-old question: *When are you going to give up that vagabond lifestyle and come back home to work for the company where you belong?*

Gee. He could hardly wait. *Not.*

So an afternoon spent with a beautiful young woman whose gold-tinted brown eyes actually sparkled as she looked in delight at the softly falling snow sounded like a great idea to him. The best one he'd had in ages—the last being when, after graduating from Illinois State, he'd decided to come to New York for a while rather than going home to work for Elite Construction. He didn't regret that decision. Especially today. Today, he was very happy to be right where he was.

"Do you want me to carry that?" he asked as they snaked up the street, weaving around street vendors and harried shoppers.

Lucy glanced down at the rumpled box containing her broken gift from her brother. She was still clutching it against her chest. Every once in a while, a distinctive tinkle of broken glass came from within. Each one made her wince.

His hands reflexively curled every time he saw her pain. He so should've laid-out her jerk of an ex. "Are you okay?" he asked, stopping in the middle of a sidewalk, earning glares from a dozen people who streamed past them.

She nodded. "I'm fine, really. Thanks for the offer, but I'd rather hold onto this for a while."

She'd probably like to find a quiet place where she could open her gift, but that wasn't going to happen here.

Taking her arm as they were nearly barreled into by a power broker yammering into his cell phone, he led her down Broadway. Manhattan at Christmastime was a world of mad colors, sounds, and crowds, and this area felt like the pulsing center of everything. It might not have all the high-end shop windows up on Park or Fifth, with their fancy displays that dripped jewels and overpriced designer clothes. But it had a million little electronics stores with huge Sale signs in their windows, kitschy tourist shops, street performers, barkers, camera crews and vendors selling everything from scarves to hot dogs.

It also had so much life. Walking one block up Broadway brought words from a half-dozen languages to his ears. While the city often got a bad rap for being unfriendly, Ross had never heard so many Merry Christmases. Even Lucy, who'd sworn she was a Scrooge about the holidays, seemed caught up in it.

"This is the worst place in the world to be today, you do realize that, right?" she said, laughing as they wove through a crowd of Japanese tourists loaded for bear with shopping bags.

They'd just headed down into a subway station, Ross having suddenly realized exactly where he wanted to go. "Nah. Maybe the second worst. Just wait till we get to our destination—that's number one."

"Uh-oh. Dare I ask?"

Grinning, he remained silent as they crammed into the subway car. Despite her pleas for clues, he didn't say anything, not until they were actually across the street from the store he most wanted to visit. Then he pointed. "We're here."

Her jaw unhinged. "You've got to be kidding! You seriously want to go into the biggest toy store in the universe *today?*"

"Come on, it'll be fun."

She took a step back. "It'll be insane. There will be a gazillion kids in there."

"Nah. Just their frenzied parents."

"Who are worse than the kids!"

"You'll like this, I promise. Come on, Miss Cranky Ass."

She gaped.

"Look, I need to get a present for my nephew. I know he'd love this walking, roaring dinosaur toy I've seen commercials for. My sister told me he's spent the last month with his arms hidden inside his shirt, waving his little hands and roaring at all his preschool classmates."

"Velociraptor?"

"Yup."

"Okay, at least he's got good taste in dinosaurs. They're my favorite, too."

"I always preferred the T-rex, myself."

"Not bad," she said with a shrug. "So I guess that means we're a couple of carnivores."

He nodded, liking the banter, especially liking that the bad mood her ex had caused appeared to have completely disappeared. "I guess so. Though, I don't suspect it would take a whole pack of you to bring me to my knees." No, he suspected Lucy would be quite capable of that all on her own.

He didn't elaborate, letting her figure out what he meant. When she lowered her lashes and looked away, he figured she had.

What could he say? He was affected by her, had been at first sight. The feelings had grown every minute they'd spent together. Not that she was probably ready to hear that from a guy she'd met a few hours ago. Nor, honestly, was he ready to say it. Knowing she was amazing, fantastic—and that he wanted her, badly—was one thing. Admitting it this soon was another.

So he went back to safer ground. "Anyway, that store's probably the only place I'm going to find the dino-toy I'm looking for today. It walks, it roars, he'll love it!"

"Preschool-age appropriate?" she asked, sounding dubious.

"Hell, no." He grinned. "But that's for his parents to deal with. I'm just the cool uncle who buys it."

Considering the present might be late, he wanted to make it a good one. No internet gift card could ever satisfy a four-year-old, and since Ross was the boy's godfather, and his only uncle, he had to do right by him.

"So, what do you say?"

"I dunno…"

"We're talking about going into FAO Schwarz, not Mount Doom and the fires of Mordor."

She rolled her eyes. "At least there are no screaming little ones on Mount Doom, unless you count the Hobbits."

He liked that she got the reference. He wasn't a total geek but couldn't deny being a LOTR fan. "None in there, either. They're all home being extra-good, hoping Santa will notice."

"How about I wait outside?" she offered, looking horrified by the idea of going in, but also a bit saddened by it.

Lucy was obviously serious about that not-liking-Christmas thing. Though, he wondered if it was the holiday she didn't like, or the memories that were attached to it. Given the few things she'd said about her parents, and the happy childhood she'd had before she'd lost them, he suspected that might be it.

Well, bad memories never truly went away, but they could certainly be smacked into the background by good ones.

"Your call," he replied, tsking. "But remember, you don't have to shop. Don't you think you'd have fun watching the crazed parents fighting over the last Suzy Pees Herself doll, or the My Kid Ain't Gonna Be Gay Monster Truck playset?"

Lucy laughed out loud, as he'd hoped she would. "When you put it that way, how could I possibly refuse?"

"You can't. Anyone with an ounce of schadenfreude in their soul—which I suspect you have, at least when it comes to Christmas and oddly-penised exes—would race me to the door."

Mischief danced on her face and a dimple appeared in her cheek as she offered a self-deprecating grin. She didn't deny it. That was something else he liked about her. Most other women he knew kept up that I-love-puppies-and-kitties-and-everyone front, at least at the beginning of a relationship. Lucy hadn't bothered. Hell, she freely admitted she hated Christmas, and had been fantasizing about cutting off a guy's dick when they'd met. Talk about not putting on some kind of nice-girl act. Was it any wonder he already liked her so much?

"Okay, Mount Doom, here we come," she said, taking his hand.

It was cold out—very cold—yet neither of them wore gloves. His were tucked in his pocket, and he knew she had some, too, since she'd worn them when they'd first left the coffee shop. But neither of them had put them on once they'd left her ex's place…once she'd taken his hand. Her fingers were icy cold, and he suspected his were too. But it was worth it.

Slowly making their way through the crowds outside, they ventured into the hell that was called a toy store the day before Christmas Eve. The moment they entered, they were assaulted with heat and noise and color. Any kid would have thought they'd entered wonderland—the whole place was set up to inspire thoughts of childhood fantasy. Well, if your fantasy included being pressed jaw-to-jaw with strangers. Oh, and getting into the spirit of the season by elbowing each other to get closer to the front of the long lines at the cashier stations.

"You've got to be kidding me!" she said when she

realized it was worse than she'd predicted. Not a square foot of floor space seemed to be unoccupied. The merriment from outside hadn't worked its way in here. These people were shopping like they were on a mission: *Nobody gets between me and my Bratz dolls.*

"I think we've just entered shark-infested waters," she said, raising her voice to be heard over the loud music and the general thrum of too many people packed in too small a space.

"Stick close to me, minnow."

"Gotcha, big white. But please tell me this dinosaur you're looking for isn't the hottest toy of the season."

"Nah, that's the Suzy Pees Herself *and* Drives a Monster Truck doll."

"My kind of girl. Uh, other than the peeing herself part."

"Whew!"

Finally, after one too many stomps on her foot, Lucy reminded him she wasn't the one shopping. She ducked into a corner and waved him off. Every time he caught sight of her, watching the hysteria that surrounded her, he noted the expression on her face—amusement, yes. But also, he suspected, relief that she didn't have to actually be a part of this.

Maybe one day she'd want to. One day when she didn't have just her brother, and a single broken gift to look forward to for the upcoming holiday weekend.

And me.

Ross was reaching around a glowering man—who was arguing with a sharp-tongued woman over what was apparently the last Barbie doll in Manhattan—when that realization struck him. He was here, alone, with plans to do nothing more than eat Chinese food and watch *National Lampoon's Christmas Vacation* this weekend. And Lucy was going to be here alone, too.

His mind didn't go where it might have gone a year or two ago, when he'd been more focused on what happened at the end of a date with a girl than during it. He didn't immediately picture the two of them naked under the mistletoe.

Well, it wasn't the *only* thing he pictured when he thought about spending Christmas with her. But mainly, he thought about seeing her smile, hearing her laugh, touching her soft skin and that amazing hair. Even if they spent the weekend pretending Christmas didn't exist, he really wanted to spend it with her.

After some hunting, Ross found the Robo-Raptor toy he'd been seeking. The thing was expensive, but, considering it would likely be late, he wasn't going to quibble over the cost.

Grabbing it, he made his way back to Lucy, finding her not too far from where he'd left her. She stood by herself, having found another quiet corner, and was gazing at a display in the games area. A huge Candyland display, with nearly life-size gingerbread men game pieces and tons of pink fluff that looked like cotton candy.

Lucy's expression was definitely wistful. As he watched from several feet away, she reached out and touched a large fairy-type doll—he couldn't remember the name, it had been a long time since his board game days. Her hand shook slightly, but the touch on the pale blue hair was tender. Sweet. As if she were reaching out and stroking the gossamer wings of a beautiful memory that flitted in her subconscious. Having noticed the hint of moisture in her eyes, he suspected she was.

As he approached, he noticed her reach up and swipe at her face with her fingertips, confirming that moisture had begun to drip. Ross dropped a hand on her shoulder. "You okay?"

She nodded. Her voice low, she explained, "This is so pretty. I loved this game as a kid."

"I was more of a Chutes and Ladders fan, myself."

She barely smiled, and he regretted making light of it when something was on her mind.

As if knowing he was curious, she admitted, "I used to beg my mother to play with me all the time. She ran the business with my Dad, and had more time at home than a lot of moms, so I assumed that meant she was mine 24/7."

"I think every kid feels that about their mom."

"Well, I was pretty relentless, and eventually we had to start negotiating. 'Just let me finish this paperwork, and I promise we'll play *one* game of Candyland.'"

"Kinda like how my parents negotiated with me—eat one more green bean and you can have ice cream after dinner."

She nodded. "Exactly. I outgrew the game, of course, but one day when I was older, it occurred to me that every time we had played, I would *always* get the Queen Frostine card within the first couple of hands. So I always won."

He glanced at the board on display, seeing how close that particular character was to the winning space, and smiled slightly. "Quickly."

She laughed. "Exactly. I was a world champion Candylander. My mom was a world champion cheater for fixing the deck so I'd get that card and win the game super-fast every time."

"Did you confront her about it?"

"Uh-huh. When I was eleven or twelve." Her laughter deepened. "She totally confessed, saying she'd never break a promise to me, and always played when she said she would. But that didn't mean she couldn't speed up the process a little."

Her eyes, which had been sparkling with tears a few minutes ago, now gleamed with amusement. The warmth of the good memory had washed away, at least temporarily, whatever sadness she'd been feeling.

"I miss her a lot," she admitted simply. "My dad, too. It'll be five years Tuesday."

He sucked in a surprised breath. She'd lost both parents, together, which could only mean some kind of tragedy. And just two days after Christmas... No wonder she'd just rather skip over the whole holiday season. Talk about mixing up happy thoughts with sad ones. "I'm so sorry, Lucy."

"Me, too." She glanced around the crowded store. "I guess you've figured out that's why I'm not a big fan of the season."

"Yeah."

"That's why my brother and I have unconventional holidays."

But this year, she'd already told him, she wouldn't be seeing her brother. And her roommate was going away. She would be entirely alone, surrounded by a merry world while she sunk deeper into memories of the past.

Not if he could help it. She wanted unconventional? Fine. One good way to start—how about Christmas with a near-stranger?

He lifted a hand to her face and brushed his fingertips across her cheek. "Well then, how about we make a deal? I promise not to sing any carols or serve you any eggnog…if you promise to spend this holiday weekend with me."

A FEW HOURS later, after having shopped a little more and laughed a lot more, they grabbed some dinner, then headed back toward Lucy's place. The tiny apartment she shared with Kate wasn't too far away from Beans & Books, where Ross had left his truck. She told herself he was just escorting her home and would then leave. But in the back of her mind, she couldn't help wondering just how *much* of the weekend he'd meant when he talked about them spending this holiday together.

And how much she wanted him to mean.

It was crazy, considering she'd dated Jude for three months and had barely let him onto second base, with one unsatisfying attempt to steal third. But she already knew she wanted Ross to hit the grand slam. What she felt when she was with him—savoring the warmth of his hand in hers, quivering when his arm accidentally brushed against her body, thrilling to the sound of his voice—was undiluted want. She'd heard it described, but now, for the first time, she *felt* it.

She knew she should slow it down. But something— not just the instant physical attraction, but also his warm sense of humor, his generosity, the sexy laugh— made him someone she didn't want to let get away. So, when they got back to her building, she intended to invite him up for a drink. And then see what happened. Or make something happen.

She and Kate shared a small efficiency, whose rent was probably as much as a mortgage payment for places outside the city. Right now, the apartment was empty. Kate had left for the holidays—she'd called two hours ago, right before Teddy was picking her up. So the place was all Lucy's for the weekend.

Hmm. Was it possible she was within hours of getting *it* at last? She didn't mean getting laid, she meant finally understanding. Finally grasping what it was like to be so overcome by pleasure that you lost track of the rest of the world.

Her steps quickened. She was so anxious to get home, to start finding out if the weekend included nights or only daytime hours, she didn't notice when Ross stopped walking. She finally realized it and looked over her shoulder, seeing him a half-dozen steps back. He stood in the middle of a crowded Sixth Avenue sidewalk, and was gazing up toward the sky.

No. Not the sky. Those twinkling lights weren't stars. Instead, thousands of tiny bulbs set the night aglow, their gleam picked up by a sea of sparkling ornaments gently held in the arms of an enormous evergreen.

"Can you believe this is the first time I've seen it?" Ross asked, staring raptly at the Rockefeller Center Christmas tree.

"Seriously?"

He nodded. "It's my first Christmas in the Big Apple, and I haven't happened to be over this way for the past few weeks."

Lucy might be Ebenezer's long-lost twin sister, but she couldn't be a scrooge when it came to seeing Ross with that delighted expression on his face. He looked like a kid. A big, muscular, incredibly handsome, sexy-as-sin kid.

She returned to his side, looking up at the tree. It was beautiful against the night sky, ablaze with light and color. Even her hardened-to-Christmas heart softened at the sight.

Saying nothing, Ross led her toward an empty bench ahead. It was night and the crowds had thinned to near-reasonable levels.

She sat beside him on the bench, giving him time to stare at the decor. But to her surprise, he instead looked at her. "Since this is probably as close to a tree as you're going to get this year, do you want to open your present now?"

She glanced at the tattered box, which she'd lugged around all day. She could wait and open it when she got home, but somehow, this moment seemed right. "I already know what it is."

"Really?"

"Well, not specifically." She began plucking the still-damp packaging paper from the box. "Sam and I have this tradition."

"I suspect it's a nontraditional one."

"You could say that." She actually smiled as she tore off the last of the paper and lifted the lid. Jude might have broken her gift, but it was the joy of seeing what Sam had found that delighted her. No broken glass could take that away from her.

"Oh, my God," Ross said, staring into the mound of tissue paper inside the box. "That is…is…"

"It's the ugliest thing I've ever seen," Lucy said. She lifted her hand to her mouth, giggling. Jude's petty destruction hadn't done much to make this thing less appealing, because it had already been pretty damned hideous. "Isn't it perfect?"

His jaw dropped open and he stared at her. "Seriously?"

"Oh, yeah," she said with a nod. Then she lifted the broken snow globe, now missing glass, water and snow, and eyed the pièce de résistance that had once been the center of it. Sitting on a throne was the ugliest Santa Claus in existence. His eyes were wide and spacey, his face misshapen, his coloring off. His supposedly red suit was more 1970's disco-era orange, and was trimmed with tiny peace signs. Beside him stood two terrifyingly emaciated, grayish children who looked like they'd risen from their graves and were about to zombiefy old St. Nick.

Hideous. Awful.

She loved it.

"Oh, this is so much better than what I got him—a dumb outhouse Santa complete with gassy sound effects."

"Do you always give each other terrible presents?"

"Just for Christmas. He gives me snow globes, I give him some obnoxious Santa, often one that makes obscene noises."

He chuckled. "My sisters would kill me if I did that."

"It started as a joke—a distraction so we wouldn't have to think too much about the way it used to be. And it stuck."

She couldn't be more pleased with her gift—unless, of course, it weren't broken. But she wouldn't let Sam know about that part. The center scene was the key.

Smiling, Lucy tucked the base of the globe back in the box, trying to avoid any bits of glass. But when she felt a sharp stab on her index finger, she knew she hadn't been successful. "Ow," she muttered, popping her fingertip into her mouth.

"Let me see," he ordered.

She let him take her hand, seeing a bright drop of red blood oozing on her skin.

"We should go get something to clean this."

"It's okay, we're not too far from my place…as long as you're ready to leave?"

He rose, reaching for the now-open box, and extending his other hand to her. She gave him her noninjured one, and once she was standing beside him, he dropped an arm across her shoulders. Ross took one last look at the famous tree. Then, without a word, he turned to face her.

"I know this is cheesy and right out of a holiday movie," he said, "but I'm going to do it anyway."

She wasn't sure what the *it* was, but suddenly understood when he bent to kiss her. People continued to walk all around them, street musicians played in the background, skaters called from the icy rink below. But all that seemed to disappear as Lucy opened her mouth to him, tasting his tongue in slow, lazy thrusts that soon deepened. It got hotter, hungrier. Both of them seemed to have lost any hint of the restraint that had kept them from getting this intense during their previous kiss.

Ross dropped his arm until his hand brushed her hip, his fingertips resting right above her rear, and Lucy quivered, wanting more. A whole lot more.

"Get a room!" someone yelled.

The jeer and accompanying laughter intruded on the moment. Sighing against each other's lips, they slowly drew apart.

"Thank you," he said after a long moment, during

which he kept his hand on her hip. "I can check that off my bucket list."

"Kissing in front of the Rockefeller Center Christmas tree?"

"No. Kissing *you* in front of the Rockefeller Center Christmas tree."

She couldn't keep the smile off her face as they began walking the several blocks to her apartment building. Ross carried not only the bag with his robotic dinosaur, but also her snow globe. He had insisted on wrapping a crumpled napkin around her fingertip, but she didn't even feel the sting of the cut anymore. Because the closer they got to home, the more she wondered what was going to happen when they arrived. That kiss had been so good, but also frustrating since she wanted more.

Much more.

Unfortunately once they reached her building, and she looked up and saw what looked like every light in her apartment blazing, she realized she wasn't going to get it. Damn. "I guess Kate didn't leave, after all," she said, wondering why her friend had stuck around. It was nearly 10:00 p.m.; Kate and Teddy were supposed to get on the road hours ago.

"Your roommate's still here?"

"Sure looks like it. No way would she leave all the lights on—she's a total nag about our electric bill."

Ross nodded, though he averted his gaze. She wondered if it was so he could disguise his own disappointment.

It wasn't that she hadn't had dates up to her place before; Jude had been over numerous times. It was just, she'd wanted to be alone with Ross. *Really* alone.

And there was no privacy to be had in her apartment. She slept in one corner on a Murphy bed, with just a clothesline curtain for a wall, and Kate used the daybed that doubled as a couch the rest of the time.

Being with him in a confined space, under the amused, knowing eyes of her roommate, would be beyond torturous.

He seemed to agree. "What time should I come tomorrow?"

She raised a brow.

"You promised me the holiday weekend, remember?"

"You really meant that?"

He lifted both hands and cupped her face, tilting it up so she met his stare. "I absolutely meant that."

Then he bent down and kissed her again. He kept this one light, sweet, soft. Still, Lucy moaned with pleasure, turning her head, reaching up to tangle her fingers in his hair. Once again, the damned box was between them, and now, a dinosaur was, too. But maybe that was for the best. Kissing him—feeling the warm stroke of his tongue in her mouth—was too exciting. If his hot, hard body were pressed against her, she'd be tempted to drag him up the stairs and see just how much privacy a clothesline curtain offered.

Ross ended the kiss and stepped back. "Good night, Lucy Fleming. I'm really glad I met you."

"Ditto," she whispered.

"See you tomorrow."

"Tomorrow."

Then, knowing she needed to get away now, while she had a brain cell in her head, she edged up the outside steps. She offered him one last smile before jabbing her finger on the keypad to unlock the exterior door, then slipped inside.

Her heart light as she almost skipped up the stairs, she felt like whistling a holiday tune. For the first time in several years, Lucy was actually looking forward to Christmas Eve. Because she had someone so special to share it with.

As she opened the apartment door, she looked around the tiny space for her roommate. "I thought you'd be long gone by now," she called.

Kate didn't respond. Lucy walked across the living room to the galley kitchen, peering around the corner, seeing no one. Then she noticed the thin curtain that shielded her bed from the rest of the apartment shimmy. *Strange.* "Katie?"

The curtain moved again, this time fully drawning back. Lucy's mouth fell open as she saw not her pretty roommate but someone she'd truly hoped to never see again. "Jude?"

"Where have you been? I've been waiting for hours."

"What do you think you're doing here? How did you get in?"

"Had a key made a couple of weeks ago." He smiled thinly, stepping closer, a slight wobble in his steps. *Drunk.* "It's my birthday. You never gave me my present. I've been waiting for it a long time and expected to get it tonight."

He stepped again. This time, Lucy saw a gleam in his eye that she didn't like. Jude suddenly didn't look like a drunk boy. More like a determined, vengeful man. One who might like her to think he was a little more intoxicated than he truly was.

She edged backward.

"Where you going? C'mon, you're not *really* mad, are you? You know I don't care anything about that skank. I was just frustrated, waiting for you. Guys have needs, you know." He stepped again, moving slightly sideways, and she suddenly realized he was trying to edge between her and the door.

This was serious. Kate was gone, her next door neighbor was practically deaf and few people were out on the street in this area this late. And Jude knew all of those things.

"I still can't believe you got some dude to come with you to my apartment," he said, his eyes narrowing and his mouth twisting. "That was wrong, to bring some stranger into this."

Ross. Oh, God, did she wish she'd invited him up!

Lucy's thoughts churned and she went over her options, none of which included intervention by a knight in shining armor, *or* a carpenter in brown leather. Her brother had drilled college rape statistics into her head before she'd ever left home. He'd also taught her a few defensive moves. But better than trying to physically fight Jude would be to get him to leave.

She began thinking, mentally assessing everything in the apartment, knowing the knives in the kitchen were none too sharp. He now stood between her and the door. Her cell phone was in her purse and they didn't have a land line—not that anybody she called, including the police, would get here for a good ten or fifteen minutes. In that time, he could do a lot. And, she suspected, that's exactly what he intended to do.

"What's the matter?" he asked, a sly smile widening that petulant mouth. "Don't you want to give me something for my birthday? After making me wait all this time, you owe me."

"I don't owe you anything," she snapped, curling her hands into fists, deciding to go for the Adam's apple.

"Yeah, bitch, you do," he snarled, the mask coming off, the pretense cast aside. Any hint of the sloppy drunk disappeared as he rushed her, the rage in his expression telling her he was fully aware and cognizant of what he was doing.

But so was Lucy. She sidestepped him, kicking at his kneecaps with the thick heels of her hard leather boots. He stumbled, fell against the daybed and knocked over a lamp.

Not wasting a second, she headed for the door, hearing his roar of rage as he lunged after her. His fingers tangled in her hair and she was jerked backward. Ignoring the pain, she spun around and slashed at his face with her nails.

"Little cock-tease," he yelled.

Then there was another roar of rage. Only this one didn't come from Jude. It came from behind her, from the door to the apartment, which she'd neglected to lock when she came in.

Ross. He was here. Against all odds, for who knew what reason, he'd come up and gotten here just in time.

Stunned, Lucy watched as he thundered past her, tackling Jude around the waist and taking him down. A handful of her hair went with them, but she was so relieved, she barely noticed.

"You slimy sack of shit!"

The two guys rolled across the floor, knocking over furniture. Jude squirmed away and tried to stagger to his feet. Ross leaped up faster, his fists curled, and let one fly at Jude's face. There was a satisfying crunching sound, then blood spurted from that perfect, surgically enhanced nose.

Jude staggered back. "Dude, you broke my nose!"

Ross ignored him, striking again, this time landing a powerful fist on her would-be rapist's stomach. Jude doubled over, then collapsed onto the day bed, wailing.

Ross gave him a disgusted sneer before turning his attention to Lucy. "Are you all right? Did he…"

"No, I'm okay," she said, shaking as it sunk in just how bad this could have been. "Thank you."

"I was a block away, when I realized I was still holding your present from your brother." He gestured toward the floor, where the package lay. "I heard yelling from outside. Fortunately I remembered the numbers you hit on the keypad."

Thank God.

"I'm gonna have you arrested for assault!" Jude raged as he staggered back to his feet.

"Okay, sure. We'll share the back of the police car as you're hauled in for attempted rape," Ross replied, fury sparking off him as he took a threatening step toward Jude.

The other man dropped his shaking hand, eyeing Lucy, his mouth quivering. "Wait, I didn't mean…I wouldn't have…"

"Yes, you would have," she replied, knowing it was true. "And I am pressing charges."

"Don't—my parents…I could lose my internship! I'm sorry, I guess I just went a little crazy."

She didn't feel any sympathy for him. But she was worried about Ross. He was a carpenter, a flat-broke out-of-towner, and Jude was the only son of a rich corporate shark. Lucy only had her word to convince anyone that Jude had attacked her.

Well, that and a probable bald spot.

She needed to think about this. "Just go," she said, suddenly feeling overwhelmed.

"Thank you!"

"I'm not promising you *anything.* At the very least, I'm reporting you to campus security and to the dean's office."

Jude's bottom lip pushed out in an angry pout. But Ross cut him off before he could say a word. "Get the fuck out, before I hurt you some more."

Shutting his mouth, Jude beelined for the door, giving Ross a wide berth, as if not trusting him not to lash out. Probably a good call, considering Ross was visibly shaking with anger.

Just before he left, Jude cast Lucy one more pleading glance. She ignored him, focused only on Ross. Her knight in shining armor, whether he saw it that way or not.

Lucy had never been the kind of girl who wanted to be rescued. Nor had she ever thought she'd need to be. But tonight, that Galahad riding in on the proverbial white horse thing had come in incredibly handy.

Once they were alone, Ross strode to the door, flipping the lock. When he returned, he didn't hesitate, walking right to her with open arms. Lucy melted against his hard body, letting go of the anxiety of the past ten minutes and just holding on, soaking up his warmth and his concern. He kept stroking her, running his fingers through her hair, tenderly rubbing tiny circles on the small of her back. Murmuring soft words into her ear.

It was, quite honestly, the most protected and cherished she'd felt in years.

"It's okay, Luce, he's gone. He's gone."

Finally, after several long moments, he pulled back a few inches and looked down at her. "You shouldn't stay here alone."

No, she probably shouldn't. "He said he made a key…"

"You're *definitely* not staying then." He mumbled a curse and stiffened, and she knew he was mad at himself for not getting the key back before Jude had left.

"I guess I could go to a hotel…"

"Screw that," he muttered, looking at her with an incredulous expression, as if she'd said something absolutely ridiculous. "Pack a bag, you're coming home with me."

7

Now
Chicago, December 24, 2011

ROSS WAS AT HIS PARENTS' house outside of the city when the call came in about Chip being taken to the hospital. The caller told him the elderly man had gone outside to deal with an accident, and the exertion of helping to push a car out of the snow had apparently caused a heart attack.

The police officer who called didn't have any more information, but that was enough to send Ross back into town. He didn't have the phone numbers of the other guards with him, nor could he be sure they'd be able to go in to the office. He had no idea whether Chip had even locked the main doors when he'd gone out to help the driver, so somebody had to get in there. And the buck always stopped at the boss's desk.

The drive would be bad, and he already knew he'd have to spend the night at the office. Fortunately Stella had made up the fold-out sofa in his office. Besides, while everyone was disappointed—especially his older sister, who'd just arrived with her family for the holidays—he couldn't deny he wouldn't mind getting away from all the holiday cheer. He hadn't been able to take his mind off Lucy, and the longer he stayed, the more likely it was somebody would notice. He just didn't feel like explaining his mood to a nosy sibling or parent.

It was nearly 2:00 a.m. by the time he arrived— the trip had taken three exhausting, stress-filled hours. The plows were barely managing to keep up with the thick snow—he'd earned a few scolding stares from their drivers as he followed them down newly plowed stretches of highway.

The private parking lot wasn't plowed, of course, and he was glad he drove a monster SUV that could clear the already foot-high drift. Parking, he bundled up, then stepped outside, his body immediately battered by the wild wind. It howled eerily in the night and the snow seemed to be moving in all directions—up, down, sideways. Not that he could see much of it in front of his face, and he suddenly realized why.

There were no lights on. Not anywhere.

Blackout. Wonderful.

Fortunately the building was well-insulated and plenty warm. He had a couple of extra blankets for the fold-out; he'd be fine overnight, and hopefully the power would be back on in the morning.

Hunching against the wind that tried to knock him back with every step, he made his way through the wet snow to the entrance, finding the doors locked. He had a master key, and used it to get in. Emergency reflective lights cast a little illumination in the lobby, and he cautiously made his way to the security desk, knowing a few industrial-strength flashlights were stored back there. Grabbing one, he headed for the stairs, trudging back up six flights, mere hours after he'd raced down them. Going up definitely took longer.

By the time he got to his floor, he was ready for sleep. It looked like he might be snowed in for a couple of days, so he'd have plenty of time to work. Right now, he was weary—physically and emotionally—and just wanted to call it a night.

Once inside his office, in familiar territory, he turned off the flashlight. Hopefully the power would be on tomorrow, but if not, he wanted to conserve the battery. Stretching, he stripped off his wet coat and kicked off his shoes, then walked across the office to the small, private sitting area.

Ross moved cautiously; it was even darker in this corner, since there were no windows. He still managed to bump into the edge of the fold-out, and muttered a curse. Then, glad the day was over, and that it couldn't get any crazier, he lifted the covers and climbed into the bed.

A noise split the silence. A low sigh.

What the hell?

The sound surprised him into utter wakefulness. Carefully reaching out, he patted the other side of the bed…and felt a body under the covers.

"Ross?" asked a soft, sleep-filled woman's voice.

A familiar woman's voice.

"Lucy?" he whispered, shocked.

Could it really be her? He knew that voice, and could now smell the sweet cinnamon-tinged scent she always wore.

She mumbled something and shifted, scooting closer as if drawn to his warmth. His eyes had adjusted a little, and he was able to make out her beautiful face. The creamy skin, the strand of dark hair lying across her cheek, the perfect mouth drawn into a tiny frown.

And she'd said his name in her sleep.

His heart pounded as he realized it was real. Lucy Fleming was asleep in his bed, in his office, in a building that was supposed to be deserted. It made absolutely no sense, was probably the last thing he'd ever have expected to happen. Considering how determined she'd been to get away without even talking to him earlier, climbing into this bed and finding the real live Santa Claus seemed more likely.

He frantically thought of the scenarios that might have landed her here. She had to have come back sometime after the building closed—when he'd left at seven-thirty, everybody had been gone except the guard. Why she'd returned, he had no idea. Maybe she'd forgotten something? Whatever the reason, Chip had to have let her in, probably recognizing her from this afternoon.

Beyond that…what? Had she offered to stay in the building when he was taken away by ambulance? That sounded incredibly far-fetched, and the officer who'd called hadn't mentioned it.

The doors. Shit. When the locking mechanism was engaged, they couldn't be opened, even from the inside, without a key. If Chip had gone out to help the motorist, he must have locked up behind him.

"You got locked in," he murmured, suddenly understanding.

And she had no way to call for help. The building was notorious for its poor cell phone reception even in the best weather, and the phone system fed off the power, so regular phones wouldn't have worked. The internet would be out, of course, plus all the computers in the building were password protected.

He could almost picture Lucy banging on the doors, trying to get someone's attention. But with the dark night, the swirling snow and the lack of people venturing out, it must have seemed like a hopeless proposition. She'd have known she was stuck here until at least morning.

So, like Goldilocks, she'd found a bed and crawled into it.

He was glad he hadn't followed his first instinct, leaped to his feet and bellowed, "Who's that sleeping in my bed?"

Lucy Fleming is who's sleeping in my bed.

A smile tugged at his mouth. What were the odds? Six years ago tonight she'd slept in his bed, too.

Remembering everything about that night—seeing the parallels—he had to laugh softly. If he were a more new age kind of guy, he might see fate having a hand in this. But being a realist, he knew the fault lay with a blizzard, a blackout and a strong security system.

That didn't, however, mean he wasn't thankful as hell for it, as long as Chip was going to be okay. Because, trapped as she was with him in this building, it wasn't going to be easy for Lucy to walk out of his life again.

He could hardly wait until morning to see just how much snow had fallen. How long they were going to be stuck here.

And what Lucy would have to say about it.

LUCY WAS HAVING THE NICEST dream. In that state between asleep and awake, she somehow knew it was a dream, but didn't want to give it up.

She was lying on a beach, cradled by soft, sugar-white sand. The turquoise waters of the Caribbean lapped in gentle waves, caressing her bare feet, the crash of the surf steady and hypnotic. Above, the sun shone bright in a robin's egg blue sky. Occasionally a puffy white cloud would drift across it, providing a hint of shade, but mostly she just felt warm and content.

Except her nose. That was really cold.

Actually, so were her cheeks. She lifted a hand, pressing her fingers against her face, wondering how her skin could be so cold when she was lying in such deliciously warm sunshine.

Beside her, a man groaned, as if he, too, was loving the feel of the sun, and the island breeze blowing across his skin. The sound was intriguing, and she moved closer. He was hot against her, big and powerful, with sweat-slickened muscles that she traced with her fingertips. She kept her eyes closed, not needing to see his face, somehow sensing she already knew who it was.

Or, maybe a little afraid she wouldn't see the face she wanted to see.

"Mmm," she moaned as she pressed her cheek against his chest. Languorous heat slid over her; she was lulled by his rhythmic exhalations, and by the sound of his steadily thudding heart.

Wait. Too scratchy. He should be bare-chested.

She waited for the dream to change, waited for the feel of slick, male skin against her face. Instead her cheeks just got colder, and the texture against her jaw scratchier. Not smooth, slick skin. Something like… wool?

Though she desperately wanted to grab the dream and sink into it again, she'd passed the tipping point into consciousness and knew it was no use. The dream was over. She was awake. Her face was cold because she was trapped in a building with no power and no heat. It was scratchy because...because....

She opened her eyes. Waited to let them adjust to the darkness. Saw a shape. A body. A scratchy sweater on which her cheek had been resting. A neck. A face. *Oh. My. God. Ross. Ross?*

She froze, unable to move a muscle as she tried to understand. She'd gone to sleep alone, worried, angry, wondering what would happen tomorrow if nobody came to check the building.

And had woken up in bed with Ross Marshall.

It was him, no doubt about it. The guy who'd broken her heart, the one she'd sworn would never get close enough to hurt her again, was sleeping beside her in the fold-out bed! Not just beside her, but practically underneath her. Apparently, in her sleep, she had curled up against him, raising one leg and sliding it over his groin, her arm draped across his flat stomach, her face nestled in the crook of his neck.

She was practically humping the guy.

And he was sound asleep.

Lucy's first instinct was to leap up and run. Her second, to grab a pillow and beat him over the head with it, demanding to know what the hell he was up to.

But then her brain took over.

Because, as far as she could tell, Ross hadn't been *up* to anything except sleeping. She'd been the one getting all creepy-crawly, sucking up his warmth while she'd dreamed of exotic beaches and blazing sunshine. Probably not too surprising, considering Ross was still just about the hottest man she had ever laid eyes on.

Even in the nearly pitch-black room, it was impossible to miss the sensual fullness of his mouth, the slashing cheekbones, that angular, masculine face. His lashes were sinfully long for a guy, hiding those jewel-green eyes.

All the coldness she'd been feeling, at least on those parts, which weren't covered by Ross, dissipated. There was only warmth now. In fact, certain places of her anatomy throbbed with it.

She was suddenly very aware of the position of her arm across his waist, how it dipped low on his hip. Her leg had slipped so comfortably between his, she was almost afraid to move, lest she wake him. But staying like this was torturous.

Because it was simply impossible to have her legs wrapped around him, to feel him pressed against her, without remembering the past; all the ways he'd delighted her, pleasured her, thrilled her. The man had taught her things about her body she hadn't even known were possible.

While one day ago she would have sworn she was not the least bit susceptible to him anymore, the woman who'd had to get herself off in the bathtub a few hours ago would say otherwise. As would the one who now felt totally at the mercy of her girl parts.

Her nipples were tight and incredibly sensitive against his chest. The barest movement sent the fabric of her soft sweater sliding across them, and since she'd been in a hurry and hadn't grabbed a bra, the sensation was definitely noticeable.

That wasn't all. Her thighs were quivering, and between them, her sex was damp and swollen. The urge to thrust her hips nearly overwhelmed her, and she had to forcibly remind herself it was not polite to rub up against a sleeping man just to get a little satisfaction.

Though, to be totally honest, she suspected—no she knew—he could give her a *lot* of satisfaction.

She closed her eyes, took a deep steadying breath, willed her body into standby, then tried to extricate herself. Bad enough to have to wake him up and ask him what the hell he was doing here—or explain the silly story about why she was. But to do it when he knew she'd been using him as both a heating blanket and a potential sex toy was more than she could stand right now.

Holding her breath, she lifted her bent leg, drawing it back off his groin. Slowly, oh, so carefully. But when she shifted a little too low, and her jean-clad thigh brushed against the money-spot on the front of his trousers, she stopped with a gasp. Because those trousers were not flat anymore. Definitely not.

He was hard, erect, aroused.

And, she greatly feared, awake.

He confirmed it by dropping a big hand onto her arm, holding her right where she was—right against him.

"Stop."

"Uh…how long have you been awake?"

Please don't say long enough to know I've been climbing all over you in your sleep. Though, judging by the ridge in his pants—the big, mouthwatering ridge— that seemed pretty certain.

"I just woke up a few seconds ago," he claimed.

He could have been telling the truth, the gravelly note in his voice hinted at sleep. So maybe his body had just been doing its nocturnal thing. Perhaps the fact that her thighs were spread and practically begging to be parted further didn't factor into the big erection pressing against the seam of his pants.

Stop thinking about his pants. And what's in them.

Yeah, fat chance of that. Every cell she had was on high alert, and her blood roared through her veins. She might have told herself a thousand times that she never wanted to see Ross again. But being here, in his arms, knowing his body was reacting to her even if his mind didn't know it, was the most exciting thing she'd experienced in ages.

There was no sense denying it, at least to herself. She wanted him. Against all reason and all common sense.

Or maybe not. What if it *was* reasonable? Maybe it made *perfect* sense to take this unexpected moment and wring whatever she could from it.

She and Ross had been a perfect sexual match once. Lucy had spent six years learning that was a pretty rare thing. Other men had given her orgasms…nobody else had made the earth shake. Plus, she was no longer the inexperienced twenty-two year old who confused sex with love. She and Ross didn't need to love each other to experience pure, undiluted pleasure in each other's arms.

At least…as long as he *wanted* to. His body apparently did, but his mind had to be engaged in the decision-making process. Ross had walked away without a backward glance once before, so maybe this tension she was feeling didn't mean as much to him as it did to her. If not, she needed to know that before deciding whether to slide onto him and kiss his lips off, or roll over, get out of the bed and demand that he let her out of the building. Facing a blizzard sounded more appealing than admitting she wanted him and finding out he didn't really feel the same.

"You could have woken me up when you realized I was here. Why didn't you?"

"Maybe because I just wanted to sleep with you one more time," he admitted.

Nice.

Then, with a sigh, he added, "Plus I knew if I woke you up you'd put all those defenses back into place and insist on leaving in the middle of a blizzard."

She ignored the comment, since she'd pretty much just decided to do exactly that.

"So you just crawled in and curled up next to me?"

"As I recall, you were the one doing the curling," he said, his tone lazy and amused. Which confirmed he'd been awake a little longer than he'd let on. Hell.

"So," he continued, "what'd you forget?"

"Excuse me?"

"I think I put everything together—you must have forgotten something this afternoon, come back to retrieve it, then gotten stuck in the building when Chip went outside and had a heart attack."

"Oh, no! Is he okay?"

"The cop who called me said he thought he would be."

"I hope so. He was very nice, letting me come back in because, yes, I did forget something." Embarrassed to admit it, since every photographer considered their camera an extension of their own body, she explained, "I left my camera bag and my specialty lens case."

He chuckled softly, obviously reading between the lines, knowing he'd flustered her enough to make her forget her equipment. The man had always been a little too perceptive. Damn it.

This conversation wasn't going the way it was supposed to. She'd broached the topic, hoping to hear him say he'd climbed into bed with her because he wanted her so desperately.

Now they were talking about cameras and cops. Ugh.

The wind howled, and though the temperature hadn't fallen too much inside, she instinctively curled closer to Ross. They both fell silent, as if totally comfortable with the fact that they'd ended up in bed together by accident—which she still wanted to discuss, by the way.

But later. Not now. Not when he was so warm and strong, when his breath teased her hair, and his hard thigh fit so nicely between hers. Not when she was trying to breathe ever deeper, intoxicated by the warm, spicy scent of his skin.

Not when she needed to know if he really wanted her—Lucy Fleming—and not just the female body that happened to be beside him in the bed.

If he did, Lucy intended to let herself *have* him. Ross would be the ultimate Christmas present. Just this once, just for tonight.

As if he knew she had no intention of putting some distance between them, Ross lowered his hand to her wrist, lazily tracing circles on the pulse point. Like he had every right to touch her. Lucy sighed, shocked at how evocative that touch felt. Her already moist sex grew hotter, wetter, as she remembered how those strong but gentle fingers used to slide across her clit, making her come with a few deliberate strokes.

Stretching, he shifted a little, and she felt the flex of the powerful muscles in his shoulder. She'd noted earlier that his body had changed—he was bigger, broader across the chest and shoulders, though his lean hips would still be easily encircled by her thighs.

It was far too easy to visualize that. To visualize everything. In fact, she was having difficulty focusing on anything else.

Without warning, Ross moved his hand, dropping it to her hip, tugging her more tightly against his body. For warmth? For old time's sake? Because he had nothing better to do?

Oh, God, he was driving her crazy!

He continued with that steady, even breathing, remaining silent, and didn't reveal by word or deed whether he was just killing time or trying to start something.

Finally, unable to take it anymore, she sat straight up in the bed and glared down at him. "Well, are you going to do something about this?"

She was asking a lot more than that. *Are you interested? Do you feel this? Do you want me?*

He didn't respond for a second, didn't reply with a confused, *Like what?* But then, just when Lucy was about to launch herself out of the bed and call him an idiot, he moved, quickly and deliberately.

Between one breath and the next, Ross sat up, pushed her onto her back and slid over her, his powerful body pressed hard against hers. His face lowered toward her, and Lucy's heart thudded with excitement as she saw the hunger in his expression.

Then he said two words…the only two she wanted to hear.

"Hell, yes."

After that, no words were needed. Her heart flying, all thoughts disappearing, she rose to meet his lips with her own. Their tongues plunged together, frantic, hungry for a connection.

There was nothing slow and quiet about it. Only driving need and demand. Their hands raced to touch each other, and Lucy hissed when he moved his mouth to her neck and sucked her nape. He nipped lightly and she quivered, wanting that mouth, that tongue, those nibbling teeth, on every inch of her body.

The Ross she'd made love with all those years ago had been slow, tender and deliberate. This Ross was wild. Desperate. She felt his driving need, and answered it with her own. Emotion had been chased away by lust, and she realized, suddenly, that she'd been waiting for this since long before the moments they'd just spent in his bed.

She'd longed for years to feel like this, through other affairs and other men. She'd wanted to experience the intense, nearly animalistic passion she felt right now. Deep down, Lucy knew she'd been waiting for him. Ross. Waiting until they met again—as if knowing someday they would—to truly let go of every inhibition, every doubt, every question about her own desirability. To know she was someone's sexual obsession, if only for one night, one moment in time.

And she was. He wanted her with every fiber of his being. His desperate touch proclaimed it and her own body was already screaming a silent *Yes* to every little thing he might ask of her.

They separated only far enough to remove their clothes. His sweater came off, revealing the golden-skinned chest beneath, and she had to reach out and run the tips of her fingers across his impressive abs. He was built perfectly—broad chest, lean at the waist and hips. Like he'd been the model used to create the prime example of man.

When his hands touched her waist and began yanking her sweater up, Lucy arched toward him. She heard his low groan when he realized she wasn't wearing a bra, and even in the near-darkness, could see the look of pure appreciation as he visually devoured her.

Lucy had been built a little differently six years ago. She'd been more girlish, more lean. Now she was curvier, carrying an extra ten pounds in all the right places…places he obviously liked. A lot.

"God, you're gorgeous," he muttered. Then he bent to her breast, no warning, no hint, his mouth landing on her nipple and sucking hard. As if he couldn't help himself, had to quench his ravenous thirst with the taste of her.

"Oh, yes, please," she groaned.

She sunk her fingers into his hair, pressing him even harder, needing to feel it, deep down. And with every deep pull of his mouth, she did feel it. All the way down to the throbbing center of sensation between her thighs.

He leaned over to give her other breast the same attention. Plumping it with his hand, he rolled her nipple between his fingertips before he blew lightly, then suckled her. Lucy cried out at how good it felt. Savoring his attention, she kissed his neck, his shoulder, raking her nails down his bare back, wondering how he could possibly be so strong when he appeared to now be a suit-and-tie kind of guy.

She wanted to cry when he moved his mouth away again. But she got with the program when he kissed his way down her midriff to the waistband of her jeans, which he quickly unfastened. He backed away, kneeling on the edge of the bed and straightening her legs. Lucy lifted her hips, arching up toward him, helping as he tugged the denim away.

Thank God she'd been in too much of a hurry to put on long johns or something equally as hideous before she'd left home. Her pink panties weren't Frederick's of Hollywood worthy, but they were cute and sexy. And Ross seemed to like them. A lot.

Or maybe not. Because without a word, he ripped them off her, tearing the fabric. She didn't give a damn. The hunger in his every movement excited her beyond anything.

"Gotta taste you, Luce."

She had a second to prepare, then his mouth was on her, licking at her core. She actually shrieked, shocked by the raw intimacy. He didn't carefully sample her, he dove deep, thrusting his tongue into her opening, then up to her clit, then back again. She was whimpering, her hips bucking freely, helpless to do anything but take what he wanted to give. Her first orgasm smashed into her like an earthquake, making her whole body quiver. He didn't stop, merely holding her hips in his big hands, continuing to lick at her as if he couldn't get enough.

Then came the aftershocks—the tsunami—wave after wave of hot, electric delight, popping in little explosions that made her head spin. Colors, instruments, spinning lights—a whole freaking carnival seemed to be taking place all around her, all calliope music and the thrill of spinning and riding until you were breathless and just couldn't take anymore.

She couldn't take anymore.

"Stop," she ordered dazedly, knowing she'd reached that point. Pleasure overload. She could barely breathe, her heart was pounding hard enough to burst out of her chest, and she was almost hyperventilating from all the gasping.

Mostly she was stunned. Shocked.

Awakened.

They hadn't had a lot of time together six years ago, and oral sex was one intimacy they hadn't shared. She'd been young, a virgin, and he'd been tender and incredibly patient. She suspected that if Ross had ever used his mouth on her like that, she would have stalked him to Chicago.

Now, she wanted him to feel that same unadulterated freedom. Wanted to give him what she'd never given him before. Not just to please him, but also to make him as absolutely crazy as he had made her.

More, though, she wanted that intimacy for her own sake. She'd never viewed oral sex as anything more than foreplay, a tit for tat return on a guy's earlier tongue investment. This time, though, she wanted to take that thick ridge of male heat into her mouth and explore the flavors of his body. Wanted to taste him, explore him, suck his cock until his willpower gave out, or his legs did.

She scooted away, grabbing his hair and pushing him up. He eyed her from between her legs, his eyes glittering, his mouth moist. "You taste good," he growled.

Licking her lips, she murmured, "I bet you do, too."

Sitting up, she became the aggressor, stalking him to the end of the bed, until he hopped off it. Eyeing her hungrily, he said nothing as she scooted to the edge, parting her thighs around his legs.

She was eye level with that wonderful, thick ridge straining against his zipper. Though she felt just as desperate to tear his clothes away, she hesitated, holding her breath. For that moment, she felt like she was about to open a Christmas present—just one, on Christmas Eve, the way she always had as a kid. The excitement of choosing the right one, and the certainty that there would be so many more good things to come all washed over her.

Catching her lip between her teeth, she unbuttoned his jeans, then eased the zipper down. He hissed as her hands brushed against the cotton of his boxer-briefs. Burying his hands in her hair, he held her tightly, not painfully, yet more forceful than she'd ever expect from him. It felt possessive. Demanding. Unlike the tender Ross she'd known, but perfect for the hungry man who'd eaten her like he'd been served his last meal.

Pushing the jeans and briefs down, she took a second to admire his cock—strong, erect and powerful. Lucy moistened her lips, then leaned forward and kissed the tip of it, hearing him groan as skin met skin.

That groan egged her on. She parted her lips, taking him into her mouth, swirling her tongue over and over. She swallowed the hint of moisture his body released, liking the salty taste, wanting a mouthful of it. She didn't worry that taking him to the edge would cut into what she wanted from him later. Ross was young and vital, and right now he looked like he could easily do her all night long, take a coffee break, then get right back in there and bang her brains out another half-dozen times.

Her thighs clenched, moisture dripping from her sex, still swollen, maybe even a little sore, from the thorough attention of his mouth.

She gave him the same attention, sucking hard. He swayed a little, which she took as a good sign. So she took more of him, deeper into her mouth, until she could take no more. Reaching between his legs, she carefully cupped the taut sacs, timing each stroke of her hand with one of her mouth, pulling away, then sucking him deep, over and over.

His groans deepened. The pace quickened. She knew by the tenseness of those powerful muscles that he was close.

He stopped. "Uh-uh. I've waited six years. No way am I coming in your mouth."

Pulling back, he reached into his pocket and grabbed a condom. As he hurriedly donned it, she considered telling him she had the birth control covered. But she figured they should err on the safe side when they were being so impulsive, so crazy.

Ross shoved his pants completely off, then reached for her. Lucy let him lift her, wrapping her legs around his waist. He held her easily, her bottom cupped in his hands, then backed her against the wall, bracing her between it and his chest.

She sunk her fingers into his hair, tugging his mouth to hers for a deep kiss. He plunged his tongue deep… then did the same thing with his cock.

Oh, yes.

He didn't move at first, just stood holding her there, impaled on him. She felt her body soften and adjust, taking him completely. Savoring the fullness, she rocked against him, signaling him that he didn't need to go slow.

She didn't want him to go slow.

"Next time," he promised.

"Whatever," she panted

Then there were no words. Just hard thrusts of his body into hers. Deeper and deeper, he reached heights no one ever had before. Or maybe she was reaching those heights. It certainly felt like she was flying, almost out-of-body with sensation.

Moisture fell on her cheeks. Lucy realized she was crying. But not sad tears, God-it-feels-so-good-and-I've-waited-so-long tears.

She closed her eyes, dropped her head back and just took and took and took. The rocking of his groin against hers brought just the right friction and she felt all that familiar pressure boiling up again. Her clit throbbed and swelled. Then the dam burst and she came again.

"Oh, yes, God, yes."

Her words? His? Both?

She didn't know. She just knew they were both crying out, both sweating and twisting and thrusting. And finally, both coming.

He groaned, suddenly growing very still. Lucy kissed him. She could feel his pulse thundering, both against her chest, and where he was inside her, and she found herself wishing she had told him not to bother with the condom. She wanted all that heat bursting into her.

Fortunately, however, they were just getting started. They had time. Plenty of it. Because, judging by the wind battering the building, and the dark snow swirling around the windows, they weren't going anywhere anytime soon.

8

THOUGH ROSS HAD WANTED Lucy to call the police right after Jude had slithered out, he had sensed her desperation to get out of her apartment. She didn't just *want* to leave, she *needed* to. He suspected the place suddenly felt tainted to her, and had to wonder how long it would take before she ever felt safe there again.

That definitely wouldn't happen until he got her locks changed. And no way in hell was she staying there alone until then.

So, after she'd thrown a few things in a bag, they'd headed for his place. After a short walk to his truck, and a long drive out of the city, they arrived in Brooklyn. Every mile put the ugly scene further into the past, and Ross was finally able to begin clearing his mind of the mental images of what might have happened had he not shown up when he did.

The very idea made him sick. And violence surged up within him when he so much as thought Jude's name.

But now it was time to think about something else. Making sure she was okay and felt safe, for one. Wondering what the hell had happened with his life in the past twelve hours for another.

Nah, he'd think about that tomorrow.

"Here we are," he said when he pulled up outside the tiny rental house where he lived. It wasn't much to look at, but it was a place of his own—a place nobody had helped him get. He didn't love the location, but he loved not feeling like he owed anything to anybody. Especially his father.

"I can't tell you how much I…"

"Forget it," he said, waving off her thank you. Probably her twentieth since they'd left her place.

Reaching into the tiny back compartment of the truck, he grabbed her small suitcase and her camera bag, then got out, going around to open her door. She didn't wait, hopping out before he had made it around the bumper. "What a cute house!"

He raised a brow. "Seriously?"

"Sure. You have a yard and everything. I can't tell you how much I miss backyard barbecues in the summer."

"The last tenant left a grill. Maybe I'll cook up some burgers tomorrow."

She laughed. "In the snow?"

"You call this snow? Yeesh. Until you've experienced a lake effects winter, you don't know the meaning of snow."

"I have," she told him. "I grew up in Chicago."

Shocked, he almost tripped. "Seriously?" The woman he had begun to suspect was the girl of his dreams had grown up in the same city, and he'd never even been aware of her? That seemed wrong on some cosmic level.

"Uh huh. And even the thought of that windy winter reminds me why I'll never go back."

His heart twisted a little at that admission, but he pushed aside the disappointment. "Yeah, I can't say I'm missing it right now, either."

"Do you think you'll ever go back?"

"Yeah, I think so."

Actually he didn't just think it, he knew it. One of these days, he was going to have to return and face up to his responsibilities. His father wasn't getting any younger, or any healthier, and not one of his sisters showed any interest in construction.

Ross, on the other hand, genuinely loved it. He'd had a toy tool set as a kid, had built his first birdhouse at four. By the time he was ten, he had constructed a four-story Barbie house for his kid sister. He just had a real affinity for building things, and had never wanted to do anything else. Some even called it a gift.

Going away to college, then to grad school, and learning drafting and architecture had just made him better at his craft. More than that, he truly *wanted* to run the company one day, as his grandfather and now his father always said he would.

He just didn't want to be forced to work there under his father's watchful eye *now*. Having spent every summer and school holiday building things for Elite Construction, and knowing he'd end up doing that for much of his life, he just wanted some time to himself. To be free, to go somewhere new, to be totally on his own. That wasn't too much to ask, was it?

Well, it was according to his father.

"Ross?"

Realizing he'd fallen into a morose silence, he shook his head, hard. "Hold on a sec," he told her, going to the back of his covered truck to retrieve the robotic dinosaur and the bags of presents he'd been supposed to mail today. He'd told Lucy about them on the way home, and she'd promised to help him package them up tonight, then find a UPS store tomorrow.

Once inside, he flipped on the lights, and zoned-in on the thermostat. No, this wasn't a Chicago winter, but it was still pretty damn cold. Plus the house was old and drafty.

He jacked up the heat, then turned back to Lucy, who looked a lot less shell-shocked than she had when they'd left the city. He didn't try to hide his relief, glad for that strong, resilient streak he'd sensed in her from the moment they'd met.

Right now, she acted as though she didn't have a care in the world. In fact, she was wandering around, comfortable enough to be nosy and check out the house. "Oh, my God, is that really a lava lamp?"

"Like the grill, also left by a former tenant. As was the couch and the ugly kitchen table."

Lucky for him. After laying out cash for a security deposit, plus first and last month's rent, he hadn't had much money for furnishings.

Kinda funny, really, how he was living now. He'd been raised in a house with ten bedrooms on twenty acres. His sisters had each had a horse in the stable, and he'd had his choice of car when he'd turned sixteen. He hadn't necessarily been born with a solid silver spoon in his mouth, but it would have to be called silver-plated.

And now he lived in a drafty, tiny old house with hand-me-down furniture and an old analog TV that got only one station, and that only if there wasn't a cloud in the sky. He drove a five-year-old truck whose payments were still enough to make him wince once a month. Ate boxed mac-and-cheese and Ramen noodles, the way a lot of the scholarship kids in college had.

Most shocking of all? He liked it.

You do this and you're on your own, totally cut off! Don't expect a penny from me!

His father's angry voice echoed in his head. But so did an answering whisper: *But I did it anyway, didn't I? And I'm doing just fine.*

"What about the bean bag chair?" Lucy asked, interrupting his thoughts of the angry scene last summer, right after graduation, when he'd decided not to move back home.

He admitted, "What can I say? I bought that one. It seemed to go with the decor."

"Lemme guess…thrift store shopping spree?"

"Bingo." Shrugging, he added, "I was on a budget."

"I think my groovy, peace-sign Santa would fit in very well here."

"Don't even think about pawning that thing off on me. Even if it weren't broken, I wouldn't let that drugged-out St. Nick and those zombie-kids anywhere near my Christmas tree. It might lose all its needles in pure fear."

She finally noticed the small tree, standing in the front corner near the window. Her smile faded a little, as if she'd suddenly remembered it was Christmas Eve, albeit very early on Christmas Eve—only about 1:00 a.m.

It was a sad-looking thing. He'd bought it on impulse—it had been the last one on a lot up the block, scrawny and short, with half its needles already gone. It had reminded him of Charlie Brown's tree…in need of a home. So he'd shelled out the ten bucks and brought it here, sticking it in a bucket since he didn't have a tree stand.

Nor had he had any real ornaments to put on it. Right now, an empty aluminum pot-pie tin served as a star on the top, and a bunch of picture hangers and odds-and-ends hung from the few branches.

As she stared at the pathetic thing, Lucy's sadness appeared to fade. She shook her head, a slow, reluctant smile widening her pretty mouth. "Are those beer can tabs?"

"Just a few," he admitted. "I was experimenting. I'm not a big drinker, so I only had a few cans in the fridge. I finally raided my toolbox."

Putting a hand on her hip and tilting her head, she said, "And you had the nerve to criticize my Christmas decorations?"

"Hey, mine's pathetic, not terrifying."

"My snow globe from last year wasn't terrifying."

"Oh, no? Let me guess. A tiny female elf wearing pasties and a G-string?"

Her eyes rounded. "Ooh, that sounds fabulous! But, no, it was just a North Pole scene."

He crossed his arms, waiting.

"With a clown that popped out of Santa's chimney like a Jack-in-the-Box."

Shuddering, he said, "Clowns are terrifying. What's wrong with Jack?"

"Why would a Jack-in-the-Box be in Santa's chimney?"

"Why would a clown?"

"Well, that's the point," she said, laughing at the ridiculous conversation. "None of it makes any sense!"

"Which makes it perfect to you and your brother. Merry Christmas to the Scrooge siblings."

"Exactly!"

Liking that her good mood was back, he asked, "Hey, are you hungry? I've got frozen pizza, frozen bagels, frozen burgers...."

"Typical single guy menu, huh?"

"Yep. Oh, if you want some wine, I think I have a box in the back of the fridge."

She snickered.

"It was a housewarming gift from a neighbor."

One pretty brow went up. "Oh? Not a basket of muffins?"

"Let's just say my neighbor's of the cat persuasion."

Her brow furrowed in confusion.

"The cougar variety." Frankly whenever his neighbor came over, he felt like putting on another layer of clothes.

"Never mind," he said, waving his hand. "So, why don't you help yourself while I go get cleaned up."

"You look clean to me."

"Under these clothes is a layer of sawdust—I'm itchy all over. I need to take a shower."

"Help yourself," she said, waving a hand as she headed to the kitchen, already making herself at home. "Want me to make you something?"

"Whatever you're having."

"Filet mignon it is."

He snorted. "Hungry Man Salisbury steak frozen dinner, if you're lucky."

Still smiling, glad her good mood had returned and thoughts of her vicious ex—who still had a lot of bad stuff coming to him—were gone, he headed for his room. The bed was unmade, clothes draped across it, the dresser drawers open. It looked like a single guy's room. Considering he intended to offer Lucy the bed, and take the couch for himself, he took a few minutes to straighten up.

As he did so, he couldn't help thinking about how much different his life seemed now than when he'd left this morning. He'd figured he'd be coming home to a quiet house, a solitary holiday, maybe a turkey sub from Subway. And he'd been okay with that. Not happy, but okay.

But he had to admit, in recent days, as the holiday season zoomed in like a rocket ship, he had really begun to think about his family back in Chicago. He had a few friends here, but not the type you'd share Christmas with. Being from a big family—which got bigger with every sister's marriage and the births of new nieces and nephews—he began to realize there were times living alone wasn't so great. As December marched on, he'd resigned himself to a lonely, kinda pathetic holiday weekend.

Wow, did things ever change on a dime.

Still thinking about those changes, he headed into the bathroom—spent another few minutes cleaning it—then got in the shower. He hadn't been kidding about that sawdust; the stuff had filtered into his clothes as he'd maneuvered the custom-made bookcase into place at Beans & Books.

Finally, his hair damp from a quick towel-dry, he pulled on a clean pair of jeans and a T-shirt and headed back out to the living room. Smelling something—popcorn?—his gaze immediately went to the kitchen, but didn't see Lucy there.

After a second, he spotted her in the one place he had not expected her to be, doing something he had *never* expected her to do. "Lucy?"

She looked up and smiled at him, a little self-conscious. "I couldn't take it anymore, it was just sad."

Ross could only stare. It appeared she had gone all Linus on his Charlie Brown Christmas tree, and had decided to give it a little love—how appropriate for a *Lucy.* What had been just sticks, needles, picture-hangers and beer can tabs an hour ago now at least resembled a bedecked evergreen.

"Where did you…"

"I just used stuff that was lying around. Hope you don't mind, but I cut up a couple of mac-and-cheese boxes…the packets are still in the cupboard. I assume you've made it often enough that you didn't need the directions?"

"Not a problem," he mumbled, still a little shocked at how much she'd done, how quickly she'd done it, and how good it looked.

"I'm glad you're the healthy type and your microwave popcorn wasn't buttered. That would have been sticky," she said as she plucked another piece out of a bowl and stuck it on the edge of a needle. A whole thread full of them dangled on her lap. "Oh, and I hope you don't mind me digging through your kitchen drawers. I was pleasantly surprised to find that sewing kit."

"Old tenant," he murmured, still a little stunned.

"Well, thanks to the former tenant then. Unfortunately he didn't happen to leave any twinkle lights or pretty red bows behind. But luckily, I hadn't cleaned out my camera bag," she added. "I had picked up some construction paper, glitter and glue to make decorations for the studio where I'm interning."

She'd used all those things to full advantage. Right now, glittery snowmen and Santa shapes dangled from several branches, apparently with directions for making mac-and-cheese on the other side. She had also managed a long strand of construction paper garland, like the kind he'd made as a kid. Red, green and white loops encircled each other, making a colorful chain that draped around the tree.

But that wasn't all. His pot-pie pan-topper had actually been cut into a star shape. And there was some kind of red-and-white fabric tucked around the bucket, creating a tree skirt. Having no clue where she could have gotten that, he quirked a questioning brow.

She chuckled. "My elf tights. I had two pair in my bag."

Good God. Tight, shimmery fabric, usually used to encase what he suspected were a pair of beautiful legs, was now hugging a dirty bucket at the base of an old, dead tree?

"I didn't have any lights, obviously, but I think this'll work. Hold on."

He watched as she crawled around the baseboard and fiddled with something on the floor. Suddenly the tree was bathed in a soft, reddish light from below. "Glad I had the red gel on me!"

Not knowing what she meant, he bent to peer at the

light, which he realized was a camera flash with a sheet of red plastic over it.

"Voilà!"

He reached for her hand, pulling her to her feet and together they stared at her masterpiece. She'd taken a pretty pathetic stick, added a bunch of random objects and MacGyvered the whole thing into a work of art.

"Wow," he whispered, genuinely impressed. "It's amazing."

She shrugged. "But it's still not exactly traditional."

He heard the tremor in her voice and knew where her thoughts had gone—to that dirty word, *traditional*. For four years, she'd tried hard to distance herself from happy holiday traditions, keeping those sweet memories at bay for fear they'd be accompanied by sad ones. Yet now, she'd stepped out of her comfort zone, doing things she probably remembered doing with the parents she'd lost, even though it was painful for her.

And she'd done it for him.

He turned to her, dropping his hands to her waist, pulling her close to him. Lucy looked up at him, her eyes bright, shining in the holiday light, and he'd swear he had never seen a more beautiful face in his life.

"Thank you," he whispered. Then he punctuated the thanks by dropping his mouth to hers, kissing her softly.

She reached up and wrapped her arms around his neck, pressing her soft body against him. He'd kissed her earlier, but they'd both been wearing coats, and layers of clothes. Now, with just his T-shirt and her blouse, he was able to feel the fullness of her breasts against his chest. She moaned lightly, moving one leg so their thighs tangled.

As if needing to feel his skin, Lucy moved her hands under the bottom of his shirt, stroking his stomach. He pulled away enough for her to push it up and over his head, liking the way her eyes widened in appreciation as she began to explore his chest. She scraped the back of her finger over his nipple, and Ross hissed in response. This time, when he pulled her close to kiss her again, he could feel the rigid tips of her breasts, separated from his bare skin by only by that silky blouse.

Saying nothing, Lucy began to pull him with her, toward the couch. Rather than follow, he bent and picked her up. Cradling her in his arms, he crossed the room and sat down, keeping her on his lap. They never broke the kiss. It just went on and on, slow and deep and wet.

Unable to resist, Ross reached for her stomach, trailing his fingertips over the blouse, hearing her purr in response. She arched up to meet his touch, telling him she wanted more. He tugged the material free of her pants, almost shaking in anticipation, knowing he'd been dying to touch her since they'd met.

As he'd expected, Lucy's body was silkier than her clothes. He took pure, visceral pleasure in the sensation, delighting in the textures against his callused hand.

"Oh, yes, more," she whispered against his mouth.

Glad for the invitation, he began to slide the buttons open, exposing more of her warm, supple skin. Lucy shifted a little, helping him tug the blouse free of her pants, so that by the time he unfastened the last button, the shirt fell open completely.

Ross stopped kissing her long enough to look at her, soaking in the breathtaking sight. Her breasts were high and round, every inch of her creamy smooth. Her lacy bra did nothing to conceal the tight, puckered nipples. And the way she arched up toward him told him what she needed.

He happily complied, covering one taut peak with his mouth, before tasting her with his tongue through the fabric.

She jerked, tangling her hands in his hair, pressing his head harder to her breast. Ross heard her tiny, raspy breaths, the little whimpers she couldn't contain, and knew she was loving every bit of this.

So was he.

With care, he lowered one of her bra-straps, releasing her breast and catching it in his hand. Her tight nipples demanded more attention, and he licked and kissed her there, sucking deep until she was squirming on his lap.

That squirming drove him a little crazy. His cock was rock-hard beneath her sexy butt, and the way she slid up and down on him told him she knew it. It also told him she wanted to keep going.

Needing to feel her heat, to see if she was as tight and wet as he suspected she was, he unsnapped her pants and slid the zipper down. He was careful in his movements, intentionally scraping his hand against the skimpy yellow panties she wore beneath. *Satin over silk.*

She didn't pull away, instead pushing against his hand, practically demanding that he touch her more thoroughly. *As though he needed to be asked?*

His mouth still on her breast, he could feel the raging beat of her heart and knew she was almost out of her mind with excitement. Breathing deeply to inhale that musky, feminine scent that practically drugged him into incoherence, he tugged the elastic away and moved his hand to the curls covering her sex. She whimpered, digging her nails lightly into his bare back. She was begging for more, though she didn't say a word.

Needing more, too, he slipped his finger between the warm, soft lips of her sex, almost groaning at how slick and wet she was.

"Oh, God," she cried, her eyes flying open. "Please, don't stop."

As if.

"Okay, time for the clothes to go," he growled.

He helped her push the pants all the way down and off, and once she was naked in his lap, he had to just pause and visually drink her in. She was perfect, from head to foot, laid out in front of him like a feast. He didn't know where to start, he just knew he already didn't want it to end.

He reached down to the front of his jeans, unfastening them, wanting to get naked and pull her leg across his lap to straddle him. Sitting there, looking up at her while she rode him sounded like the perfect way to start this night.

"Ross?" she whispered.

"Hmm?"

"Um…there's something you probably should know."

"Unless the house is on fire, there's nothing I really need to hear right now," he said as he unzipped and pushed the jeans down his hips. His body was already on fire, and as he pushed his shorts away, too, and his cock came into contact with her bare hip, he groaned.

She gasped. "Oh, my goodness."

"Give me another five minutes and it will be both *yours*, and *good*," he told her as he stopped to kiss her breast, and stroke that sweet, quivering spot between her thighs.

"Ross, uh, really, I need to tell you something."

Hearing the quaver in her voice, and feeling the slight stiffness of her body, he finally shook off the haze of lust in his head. He lifted his mouth from her perfect breast and slid his hand into safer territory down on her thigh.

"What's wrong?"

She lowered her head, eyeing him through a long strand of hair. Lucy's cheeks were pink, like she was embarrassed. Well, hell, they'd known each other less than a day and now she was lying naked on his lap. But she wouldn't be embarrassed for long, not once he showed her how much he wanted her.

"Um…I just wanted to say…"

She bit her lip, shook her head slightly. Which was when a thought—a shocking, crazy one—burst into his head. His whole body went stiff and he leaned back into the couch.

"Lucy, are you trying to tell me you've never done this before?"

A hesitation, then she slowly nodded. "That's what I'm trying to tell you."

Holy shit. She was naked in his arms, thrusting into his hand like she needed to come or die and she was a virgin?

Well, honestly, the needing to come or die made sense. Seriously, how many twenty-two-year-old virgins were out there? He'd certainly never met one. The beautiful, sexy woman had to be a seething mass of sexual frustration.

Something he could well appreciate right now.

"I mean, you said you and Jude had never...but, seriously, nobody else, either?"

"No. Never."

"That's incredible."

"I guess right around the time most girls were giving it away in the backseats of their boyfriends' cars, I was grieving and helping my brother figure out what to do about our parents' business, their house, their lives. And ours. It just sort of...never happened."

He nodded, understanding. She hadn't been thrust into the role of sexual grown-up while in high school. She'd landed in the adult world through one brutal tragedy.

That, as much as the fact that he was not a ruthless bastard like Jude, was enough to make Ross find the strength to do what had to be done. Knowing he'd have blue balls tonight, he still cleared his throat and carefully pushed her off his lap.

"Okay. It's all right, Lucy, I understand."

She grabbed his arm before he could get off the couch and head toward the bathroom for an icy cold shower.

"No, I don't think you do." Reaching for his face, she cupped his cheeks in her hands and leaned close, her soft hair falling onto his bare shoulders. "I want you, Ross. I want you to be my first. Now. Tonight."

LUCY HAD THOUGHT a lot about the moment when she'd finally have sex. She'd pictured it being with someone she knew, someone she'd dated for a long time, someone she trusted.

Well, one out of three wasn't bad, right?

She didn't know Ross that well. She'd never dated him.

But she trusted him. Oh, did she trust him.

Telling him the truth about herself hadn't been easy, but she certainly wasn't going to try to fake her way through her first time having sex. Not only was that unfair to herself, it was unfair to him. He deserved the chance to say, "Thanks but no thanks." After all, some guys just didn't seem to want to deal with the drama of it.

She would have predicted Ross wouldn't be one of those guys.

She wouldn't have predicted the incredibly tender, loving way he kissed her, then stood and took her by the hand to lead her to his bedroom. As if now that he knew the truth, the responsibility of it was weighing on him, and he didn't want a quick lay on a couch. Like she deserved the whole package, big bed and all.

The walk to the bedroom seemed incredibly long. And while her whole body was still burning from the incredible way he'd touched her, she couldn't deny a faint trepidation, the tiniest bit of self-consciousness.

After all, she was naked. He still wore jeans. And she'd just told him she was a virgin.

"It's okay," he told her when they'd reached his room, standing by his bed. He brushed her hair off her face, then touched her cheek. "It's gonna be fine."

She smiled. "Do you think I'm afraid?"

He eyed her, visibly unsure.

"I'm not scared, Ross. Maybe a little embarrassed about being so...exposed."

He stepped back and looked at her naked body, shaking his head slowly and rubbing his jaw, as if he just didn't know what to say. Then he said exactly the right thing. "If there's any such thing as a perfect woman, Lucy Fleming, you're her."

She went soft and gooey inside, everywhere she wasn't already soft and gooey. As she'd already suspected, she'd most definitely chosen well.

"Thank you."

"So don't be nervous, Luce, I won't do anything to hurt you," he added, tenderly cupping her cheek.

"I won't. I swear to you, my only fear is that it won't be as good as I've made it out to be in my head."

A slow smile curled those handsome lips upward. He shook his head, then sunk his hands in her hair and dragged her close.

"It'll be better. I guaran-damn-tee it."

He pushed her down onto the bed, and set about proving it.

Lucy honestly hadn't known sex could be both incredibly hot and amazingly tender. He kissed her deeply, slowly, like he wanted to memorize the taste of her mouth. And his hands did magical things to her, gliding across her breasts, offering her barely there caresses that left her a quivering pile of sensation.

But then, his control would slip a little. He'd groan as he nipped her breast, or shake when she reached out and brushed her fingertips against the soft head of his erection. Lucy wanted to do more, longed to explore his body, but he seemed determined to make this all totally and completely about her.

Which was wonderful…and incredibly arousing.

"Please," she said on a sob when he again teased her clit with his fingers, giving her light touches that made her long for firmer ones. Her hips thrusting, Lucy was on the verge of going over the top, she knew that from her own explorations of her body. And she was dying for it.

As if knowing he'd teased her as much as he could before she smacked him, Ross murmured something sweet and unintelligible, then slid a finger inside her. She practically cooed; the unfamiliar invasion felt *so* good. He moved his thumb back to her clit and this time, there was no teasing. Just slow, deliberate caresses, with just the pressure she needed.

Her breaths grew choppy. Sighs turned into gasps when he slid another finger into her channel, using both to stretch and fill her, even while he continued stroking her clit.

Then it came, sweet, warm relief. She quivered as the orgasm rolled over her, amazed at how much stronger it was when shared. She cried out, let her body shake and stretch, then sagged back into the pillows.

"You're gorgeous," he whispered.

"So are you," she said, absolutely meaning it. Ross's body was delicious—so hard and muscular, all power and steel. When combined with the thoughtfulness, the boyish smile, the twinkle in his green eyes, he was an absolutely irresistible male package.

She smiled at him, wrapping her arms around his neck. "I want you now."

He didn't ask if she was sure, as if knowing they were way past that. Reaching for a drawer in the bedside table, he took out a condom. Lucy caught her lip between her teeth, watching as he maneuvered the tight sheath over his thick, powerful erection. Seeing the rubber stretch to accommodate him, she felt the first thrills of nervousness. But they were immediately drowned out by utter excitement.

Just watching him sent even more heat to her sex and she had to drop her legs apart, the skin there was so engorged and sensitive. Ross looked down at her, masculine appreciation written all over his face, then moved between her thighs.

"Tell me if…"

"I will," she said, cutting him off. Then she lifted her hips, wrapping her arms around his shoulders and staring up at him.

They didn't kiss. They didn't blink. They barely breathed.

Lucy's heart skipped a beat when she felt his rigid warmth probing into her, nuzzling between her folds and into the slick opening of her body. He moved slowly, so carefully, so tenderly. Each bit of himself he gave her just made her hungry for more.

She arched her hips toward him, silently telling him to continue. Seeing the clenched muscles in his neck, the sweat on his brow, she knew he was hanging on tightly to his control.

"I'm fine," she insisted. "Please, Ross, please fill me up."

He bent to her, covered her lips with his and kissed her deeply. And with each stroke of his tongue, he pushed into her, filling her, inch by inch, until he was buried inside her.

There had been only the tiniest hint of pain; now there was just fullness. Thickness. A sense that she'd finally been made whole and didn't ever want to go back to feeling empty again. Like he was exactly where he was meant to be.

"Okay?" he asked.

"Definitely."

She slid her legs tighter around his, holding him close. Ross began to pull out, then slowly thrust back in, setting an easy pace. She caught it, matched it, giving when he took, taking when he pulled back. It was, she realized, like dancing…one step he led, then she did. Only no dance move had ever felt so good, so sinfully delicious.

"You're so tight," he groaned, picking up the pace.

She knew his control was slipping. Frankly she marveled that he'd been able to maintain it this long. Every molecule in her body was urging her to thrust and writhe, to just take in so much pleasure that she'd never remember what it was like to not feel it. She knew he had to be feeling the same.

The rhythm sped up a little, his thrusts deepening. Lucy met him stroke for stroke, clinging to his broad shoulders, sharing kiss after kiss. Reality had faded, there was nothing else except this feeling, this rightness. This perfect guy on this perfect night.

And then, the perfect moment. Warm delight spilled through her as she climaxed again, differently than she ever had before. It started deep inside and radiated out, a ripple widening into a wave.

Even as she savored the long, deep sensations, she heard Ross's shallow breaths grow louder and felt him tense against her.

"Beautiful, you're so beautiful," he muttered as he strained toward his own release.

His low cry and the deepest thrust of all signaled that he'd found it. He buried his face in her hair and continued to pump into her, as if every bit of him had been wrung dry.

Though she knew he had to be totally spent, he didn't collapse on top of her. Instead, Ross rolled onto his side and tugged her with him. They were still joined, and she slid her thigh over his hip, liking the connection.

His eyes were closed, his lips parted as he drew in deep breaths. When he finally opened them, she didn't even try to hide her smile.

"What?"

"I liked it."

He chuckled. "I'm glad."

"When can we do it again?"

His chuckle turned into a deep, masculine laugh. "Give me a half hour."

She stuck out her lower lip in a pretend pout.

"Okay, okay," he said, reaching down and stroking her hip. "Twenty minutes."

"I guess I can live with that," she said, with a teasing smile. She rubbed against him, stealing his warmth. The bedroom was cool, but she definitely hadn't noticed it before. Ross gave off a lot of heat…whether he was right beside her or across the room.

She much preferred him right beside her.

They fell silent for a few moments, just touching each other, exchanging lazy kisses. She loved the way he kept a possessive hand on her, as if making sure she didn't disappear on him.

That wasn't going to happen. Definitely not. In fact, she was already wracking her brain, wondering how on earth they could make this work for a lot longer than this one weekend. He hadn't said he wanted to, neither had she. But she definitely felt it.

Yet, she was leaving for Europe in three weeks. She'd be gone for months, then had intended to come home only long enough to graduate, then go back again.

None of that had mattered when she'd been with Jude. Not even when she'd been thinking about sleeping with him.

Now, though? With Ross? The very thought was devastating. How could she possibly walk away when, for the first time in her life, she'd met someone she wanted desperately to hold on to?

"Is there anything you need?" he whispered, his voice breaking the silence in the shadowy room.

"Like what?"

He shrugged and looked away, as if not wanting to embarrass her. "I mean, you know, are you hurting?"

"Definitely not. Honestly, I don't know that I have ever felt better." Unable to help it, she yawned. "Okay, maybe I do need something—a catnap. A twenty-minute one."

He laughed softly and tugged her even closer, until she was actually lying on his chest. He kissed her brow, stroked her hair, whispered sweet things about how good she'd felt to him.

Lucy's cheek was right above his heart and she not only heard its beat, she also felt its steady, solid thrum. His words lulled her, his touch soothed her. Quite honestly, she couldn't recall a more perfect moment in her life.

Not ever.

She only hoped there would be many more to come, and could hardly wait to see what tomorrow would bring.

9

THEY WERE SNOWED IN. Totally trapped in a world turned white.

Standing at his office window and assessing the situation Saturday morning, Ross could only shake his head in wonder. He hadn't seen a storm like this in a lot of years, probably not since he was a kid. He tried to estimate how much of the white stuff had fallen; judging by the way it climbed up the side of his SUV, he'd say at least three feet so far. And still it came down, swirling, spinning, blowing up and down and sideways.

This might be one for the record books.

"You left and took your body heat with you," Lucy grumbled from the fold-out.

"Sorry."

She'd been asleep when he'd slipped out of bed a few minutes ago. Now she was curled on the side he'd vacated, the blankets pulled up to her nose, like she was trying to suck up any residual warmth.

She looked both adorable and sexy as hell.

And a little chilly.

Though it wasn't freezing, by any means, the temperature had definitely dropped below what it normally was in the building. Not that they'd really noticed during the night. God, had they *not* noticed. In fact, Ross would have sworn there was an inferno blazing in this little corner of Chicago. Because he and Lucy had redefined hot throughout the long, erotic hours after she'd awakened to find him in bed with her.

"How does it look out there?"

Shaking off the sultry images in his mind of the ways they'd explored and pleasured each other in the darkness, he smiled. "Like Santa decided to move here and brought the North Pole with him."

"Oh, that's just perfect," she said, sounding sarcastic.

"What's the matter, did you have big plans for the day?" He somehow doubted it. Lucy didn't seem any more of a Christmas fan now than she had been six years ago.

She thought about it, then shook her head. "Actually, no. Sam's working all weekend. I was figuring on staying in, being lazy, going online and spending that money your company paid me yesterday."

Well, she couldn't do any shopping, but staying in and being lazy sounded ideal. Especially if they were lazy between bouts of being as energetic as they'd been last night.

Damn. Lucy had become a wild woman.

Seeing her shiver, he clarified that—a *cold* wild woman.

"Here," he said, walking over to the bed, carrying two cups of coffee, which he'd just brewed.

"So the power's back on?" she asked, appearing both relieved and disappointed.

"'Fraid not," he said, shaking his head. "Fortunately, we get a lot of vendors coming in here. One of them makes a battery-operated coffeemaker and suggested we get them for sites that aren't wired yet. We did—and they gave us a few for the office as a thank-you for the contract."

"Thank goodness for free samples," she said, sitting up and letting the covers drop to her lap. Ross managed to not slosh hot coffee all over her. Seeing her in the daylight—as murky as it was—was enough to make the earth jolt. Not to mention his dick.

He hadn't realized it was possible to be so insatiable about another person. They'd had sex three or four times during the night, and he was ready to have her again. It had been dark—now he wanted to watch her face pinken as she came, see the perfect body as he licked every inch of it.

"Wonderful," she murmured as she sipped, then blew on the steaming rising from the mug. "Cream, no sugar—you remembered."

"Of course I did," he murmured. He remembered everything.

It was funny, considering he'd tried so hard to put Lucy out of his mind over the years. But she'd refused to leave, haunting his memories through other women—two of them serious—and so many other changes.

Lucy glanced at him and their stares held. She didn't try to lift the blanket, didn't blush or feign embarrassment at sitting right in front of him so beautifully naked. He'd worried she would feel some kind of doubts or uncertainty in the cold light of day. But he'd been wrong. She looked confident—serene even. Like she didn't regret a damn thing.

He smiled at the realization.

"What?"

"I half expected you to leap up, wrap the sheets around your body and accuse me of molesting you during the night."

She snickered. "I think I was the one who molested you. Although, you did creep into my bed while I was sleeping."

"*My* bed, Goldilocks. Speaking of which, I don't have any porridge to offer you for breakfast, but there's a ton of leftover party food in the break room."

She didn't seem to care about the food, instead focusing on the first part of his statement. "*Your* bed? Are you serious?"

"As a heart attack."

She looked around the office, taking note of its size and furnishings. It was, he knew, probably bigger square-footage wise, and better furnished than his entire rental house had been back in Brooklyn.

"So if the bed is yours, I guess that means this office is yours as well? I mean, I don't suppose you were just sneaking into your boss's bed since you got stuck here, too?"

"It's mine," he said with a laugh. "I'm assuming you didn't notice the nameplate on the desk."

She glanced over. Even from here it was easy to make out the "CEO" before his name. Her eyes wide, she turned her attention back to him. "You really run this place?"

"I really do."

"Wow," she said, sagging back against the pillow. "I mean, I knew you were talented, but going from handyman to CEO in six years? That's pretty remarkable."

Ross put his cup down and sat in a chair opposite her. Lifting his jean-clad legs, he used the end of the foldout as a footrest, crossing his bare feet there. "Not that remarkable, really. I inherited the position. It's my family's company."

Lucy's mouth rounded into an O. "Your father…"

"Yeah."

"How is he?" she asked. "Did he…"

"Pull through? Yes, he did. It took a long time, a lot of rehab and he still doesn't have full use of his right side, but he made it." Chuckling but only half-joking, he added, "He's still the same demanding tyrant he always was."

It would take more than a massive stroke to get his old man to stop being bossy, pushy and opinionated. And Ross should know; he dealt with that bossy, pushy opinion every damn day.

His name might be on the letterhead of Elite Construction, but his dad still held a lot of shares. They'd had a few major battles once the elder Marshall had started feeling like his old self again. It had only been lately, in the past year or so, that he'd conceded Ross was doing an excellent job, and stopped questioning every little decision.

Not that Ross wasn't very grateful his dad had lived, of course. Though they hadn't been getting along at the time, he'd been shocked and devastated by his father's massive stroke six years ago. Though he'd only been fifty-five, nobody had thought he would make it, not the doctors or the industry. Nobody except his family, who knew Ross Marshall, Sr. was too stubborn to do what everyone predicted he would.

"I'm so glad he survived," Lucy murmured.

"Thanks."

He didn't doubt she meant it. But he also didn't doubt Lucy's mind had gone right where his had—to the timing of his father's stroke. She'd been there when he'd received the frantic phone call from his sister at the crack of dawn on Christmas morning. After a weekend of pure excitement and happiness with Lucy, his world had come crashing down with one conversation.

His entire life had changed on a dime. Before that, he'd known he would someday go back to Chicago and take his place beside his father in the business. But he'd thought he had time—a couple of years, at least—to live the life he wanted. Hell at that particular moment, he'd even been considering asking Lucy if she thought he might be able to pick up some carpentry work in France for a year or two. They'd gotten *that* serious *that* quickly.

Then the phone had rung. His sister's sobs had finally made sense, and he'd left for the airport right away. As much as he'd hated bailing out on Lucy on Christmas Day, she'd been completely understanding. Hell, if anyone would understand, it would be her— she'd received her own horrifying phone call one holiday season.

He'd wasted no time packing, not even a single bag. He'd been desperate to get back to Chicago, convinced his father was on the verge of death. And horrified, realizing that the last words they'd exchanged had been angry ones.

The vigil at the hospital had been long and difficult. He'd dealt not only with the worry, and with his family, but also with stepping right in to look after the company. That, in itself, had been a battle, considering he was so young. But he hadn't been about to let the whole thing founder while his father fought for his life.

Despite being so busy, he'd found time to call Lucy every day that first week—especially knowing she had a tough anniversary of her own to contend with. During each call, she'd expressed concern about his father, but inevitably the conversation would turn to her preparations for her upcoming trip. Her plans for her future. Her great life.

Then a couple of days went between his calls.

Then a week.

Then it was almost time for her to leave for her semester abroad.

And he'd stopped calling.

"I never stopped thinking about you. I swear, you were on my mind constantly." He got to the point, the main thing he wanted to say. "I'm sorry, Lucy."

"For?"

"You know what for. I couldn't stop thinking about you…but I couldn't bring myself to call you, either."

She stiffened, didn't reply for a second, then tossed off a casual, "Hey, don't sweat it. The phone lines were notoriously unreliable that year."

He saw through the feigned humor. She'd been plenty hurt yesterday; no way had she gotten over it in one single night.

But, maybe last night had at least opened her to the

possibility that he wasn't a user who'd taken her for the ride of a lifetime then dropped her flat.

"You know, I never went back to New York."

Her brow went up. "What about your house? Your things?"

"I hired somebody to take care of it that winter, once it became obvious that not only was my dad going to have a long recovery ahead of him, he would almost certainly never be able to work again."

"That must have been really tough."

"Tough doesn't begin to describe it." He swiped a hand through his hair and sighed. "Anyway, I didn't mean to get into all that. I just brought it up so I could finally tell you what I meant to tell you then and never got the chance to say."

She eyed him warily. "And that would be?"

He held her gaze, daring her not to believe him. "That I fell in love with you that weekend in New York."

She sucked in an audible breath, and slowly shook her head.

Ross nodded, not worrying about looking like a fool or fearing any kind of rejection. Maybe something great would happen between him and Lucy now. Maybe it wouldn't, and last night would be his final memory of a relationship he'd once thought would define his whole life. But no matter what, he owed her the truth about the past.

"It's true. I was crazy in love with you."

"You might have told me…"

"To what purpose?"

Rolling her eyes and looking at him like he was an

idiot, she said, "Maybe just because the words would have been nice to hear once in my life?"

He couldn't imagine no man had ever fallen in love with the beautiful woman in front of him. But he didn't particularly want to think about her with anyone else. The very idea made his stomach heave.

"Maybe I should have," he said with a simple shrug. "But I was trapped."

She tilted her head in confusion.

"Lucy, you were about to leave to go grab the world by the balls."

She didn't try to deny it, but a wistful expression crossed her face, as if she were remembering the feisty, passionate girl she'd been. One of these days, hopefully, he'd find out what had brought her back here, why she was photographing children when she'd sworn she would do anything but.

Right now, though, he had his own story to tell.

"But me? Dad was on his deathbed, my family was falling apart, and I was the one who had to hold them— not to mention this business—together." He rose from his chair and walked to the fold-out, sitting beside her and reaching out to stroke a silky strand of her hair. "My life was here. It *is* here. Yours was—" he waved a hand "—out there. We were going to be living in two different worlds and as much as I wanted you in mine, I knew that wasn't going to happen. Just because my dreams fell apart didn't mean I could ask you to give up yours."

"So…you let me go?"

A simple nod. "I let you go."

Moisture appeared in her eyes, though no tears

spilled from them. Sniffing, she curled her face into his hand, rubbing her soft skin against his.

They remained silent for a long time. The room was quiet enough that he could hear the plink of tiny, icy snowflakes striking the window. Then, with a low sigh, Lucy looked up at him and smiled.

"Thank you for telling me," she whispered.

"You're welcome."

Nothing else. No promises. No requests. It was as if they'd just wiped clean the slate and could now start again, fresh. And see where the road took them.

"I'VE GOT TO ADMIT IT, Papa Bear, this beats porridge any day."

Lucy licked a few cookie crumbs off her fingers, sighing in satisfaction at the strange Christmas Eve brunch they'd just shared. Cookies, eggnog, cheese and crackers, chips, chocolate and fruit.

The food at the party had been plentiful and delicious. It had also kept very well in the large refrigerator, which was doing a pretty good job holding its temperature despite the power outage. Though, if they were going to be stuck here much longer, they were going to have to ditch the eggnog in favor of unopened bottles of soda or fruit juice.

"I think there's even some leftover sliced turkey for Christmas dinner," he replied. "If it comes to that."

Judging by the way it continued to snow, it could definitely come to that.

She should be bothered by it. Should be worried about being trapped, should at least be freaked out about not having a spare pair of underwear—not that she expected to wear them for long.

But the truth was, she didn't care. She had no obligations to anyone else, didn't have holiday plans, other than shopping. Her brother had already been scheduled to work all weekend, and with the weather, she doubted he'd have time to even drop by before Monday or Tuesday.

So why not spend a few days trapped in a secure building with plenty of food and water, and someone to provide plenty of entertainment. If, that was, she could survive that much…entertainment.

"I guess this meets your requirements for a nontraditional Christmas, huh?"

"Hey, I ate a bell-shaped cookie, didn't I?" Then she chuckled. "Though, believe it or not, I've gotten a little less stringent about that."

"Seriously?"

"Kate has kids now, and I actually went and spent Christmas with them a couple of years ago. It was… nice."

More than nice. It had been lovely. Sweet and wholesome and fun. And yes, a bit painful. But after many years, Lucy had been able to let down her guard and let some of the magic of the season back into her heart. She wasn't ready to go out and chop down a tree or download a copy of *Now That's What I Call Christmas #948* to her MP3 player. But she could at least hum Silent Night—her mother's favorite Christmas carol— and not want to break into tears.

"You must know I'm curious…"

"About?"

"Paris. Europe. Photographing Fashion Week, landing the cover of *Vogue?*"

She sighed, remembering that girl, those dreams.

How important they'd once seemed, when she was running away from anything resembling the life she'd once had and so painfully lost. Changing her plans completely had helped her evade the memories for a little while, but not forever. Eventually she'd had to face them.

She explained that to him, as best she could, wondering if the explanation would make any sense to anybody else.

When she was finished, Ross nodded slowly. "And now that you know you don't have to go halfway across the world to keep from caring too much about anyone or anything…are you happy?"

Wow. He'd obviously read between the lines. She hadn't mentioned anything about not wanting to care about anyone. But she couldn't deny it was true.

"I'm happy," she admitted. "I love what I do—you remember how I swore I'd never work with kids?"

"Even though you were great at it."

"Exactly. I guess I was the last one to see it. But I love it, and I'm good. I've had more success with my kid portraiture than I ever did with adults. I actually had a photo in *Time* magazine last year."

He whistled. "Seriously?"

"Yep. I've had shots picked up by the AP, and magazines and catalogs. I actually just submitted a photo essay for Parents Place Magazine as well, and I'm hoping they'll take me on for more freelance work."

"Sounds wonderful," he told her, sounding like he meant it. "I'm really happy for you."

"Thanks." Suddenly remembering something, and knowing he'd be interested, she said, "Oh, guess who I ran into a year or so ago in New York?"

He raised a curious brow.

"Remember Jude the jackass?"

His sneer said he did. "Please tell me he ended up in prison being some Bubba's bitch."

"No, but his daddy did."

Ross's jaw dropped.

"His family ran one of those businesses that was 'too big to fail.' Only, it failed during the financial melt-down. Daddy went to jail, the family lost everything. Jude was very humbled—and very poor—when I ran into him."

"Couldn't have happened to a nicer guy."

Almost unable to remember the girl she'd been when she'd thought Jude could be "the one," she said, "I guess that catches you up with what's been going on with me."

And he'd already caught her up on what his life had been like. It had been full of family and work and duty. Not much downtime, from the sound of it, although he had apparently had time to start building that dream house of his—oh, she would love to see it.

As for his personal life, though she hadn't pried, not wanting to be nosy, she had sort of rejoiced when he admitted he hadn't had any romantic relationship that had lasted longer than six months. That made two of them.

"Wait, what about your brother?" Ross asked. "Does he still give you ugly snow globes every Christmas?"

She chuckled, thinking about the collection that she set out every single year. With the exception of the broken groovy Santa, she still had each and every one.

"I put out my entire collection every holiday season."

"*All* of them?" he asked, his voice soft and serious.

She knew what he was asking. Knew he wondered if she'd kept the one and only Christmas present he'd ever given her. Considering she'd been heartbroken shortly after he'd given it to her, the answer probably should have been no. But in truth, she'd never been able to part with that special gift, even though, every time she took it out of its box, she'd wondered about Ross. Where he was, what had happened to him.

Now she knew. He'd been living his life as best he could…after having freed her to follow her dreams.

"Yes, Ross," she murmured. "Every one."

"I'm glad."

"Me, too." Then, wanting to keep the mood light, she added, "The one my brother got me last year had to take the prize for kookiest ever."

"Do tell."

"Sam found one from some weird cult that believes the three wise men came from another planet. Balthazar had green skin and claws. Melchior had a spiked tail. And the other one was furry all over."

Tossing his head back, Ross laughed. "Please don't tell me the baby Jesus was an alien, too."

"No, but he looked terrified."

"Is it any wonder? I mean, with the cast of a bad episode of *Star Trek* standing over him?"

Snorting as she realized that's exactly what the three kings had looked like, she got up and began clearing away the plastic dishes they'd used for their late-morning feast. They'd eaten in the break room, since it was closest to not only all the food, but all the supplies, too.

"So, you ready to go down and check things out?" Ross asked.

They'd agreed that, after eating, they would head

downstairs to the lobby and try to get a better idea of what was going on outside. From up here on the sixth floor, it looked like they were trapped in a spaceship that had landed on a marshmallow planet.

"Ready when you are."

Though they didn't expect to get anywhere, the two of them dressed warmly. They had raided a coat closet to add layers to their own clothes. There were a few jackets, scarves and hats that had been left behind over the years—enough so that they shouldn't freeze if they dared to step outside.

Once they trudged down the six floors to the lobby, and saw that the snow had drifted almost all the way up the glass doors, though, Lucy realized they needn't have bothered.

"This is crazy!" she said, standing up on tiptoe to try to see over the white mountain. "Can you see the parking lot?"

Ross cupped his hand around a spot of glass that wasn't obscured by snow. "There are three lumps out there—I assume your car, mine and the security truck. It would take a sled and a team of dogs to get us to them, though."

Meaning, even if the power came on and the streets were cleared, they weren't going anywhere until Ross's private snow removal contractor showed up to clear the walks and the parking lot. And who knew when that would be?

"We're not going anywhere, are we?"

"Nuh-uh." He turned to face her. "Is that okay? I mean…you're not scared about being trapped here, are you?"

She scrunched her brow. "Have you turned into a cannibal sometime in the last six years?"

He wagged his eyebrows. "You complaining about what I like to eat?"

Good Lord, she was never going to complain about that for the rest of her life.

"Never mind," she said, knowing she sounded off balance.

The man was good at distracting her, putting wild thoughts in her head. He was good at a lot of things. Making her laugh, making her sigh, making her crazy. Giving her incredible pleasure.

At twenty-two, she'd found Ross Marshall to be the sexiest guy she'd ever met. Now, six years later, she knew he was more than that. Still sexy, oh, without a doubt. Probably even more so, actually, because he had a ton of confidence and a man's mature personality to go along with the looks and charm.

But she now saw him as a whole lot more than a broke carpenter with a bean bag chair and a lava lamp. He was successful, very smart, and incredibly likable. She'd seen the way he talked to all those people at the party yesterday; now, knowing he was their employer, she was even more impressed.

"Seriously, you're not too worried, are you?" he asked. "We have plenty of food, the building's secure. And I don't think it's going to get unbearably cold. If it does, we can move to an interior room with no windows."

She shook her head. "Honestly, I'm not worried. The only question is, what on earth are we going to do to occupy ourselves?"

She accompanied that question with a bat of her eyelashes.

Ross stepped closer, dropping his hands onto her hips. Even through the padding of her pants, sweater, somebody's hoodie, somebody else's jacket and her heavy coat, she felt the possessive weight of it.

"I'm sure we'll think of something."

She gazed up at him, licking her lips and smiling. "I already have thought of something."

"Oh?"

She leaned up on tiptoes, brushing her lips against his jawline and whispered, "Close your eyes."

He did. Immediately.

"Count to twenty."

"Uh…why?" One eye opened and she immediately frowned. He closed it again. "Sorry. Counting. One."

She stepped away. "No peeking. Keep counting."

"Two."

A smile crossed his face, as if he were picturing her stripping out of her clothes, laying herself out naked on the security desk. Hmm. That could be kind of interesting. Though they couldn't possibly be seen through the drifts or the still-falling snow, it sounded extremely daring.

"Three."

She shook her head and tiptoed backward toward the closed stairwell door. He was saying four as she carefully pulled it open and five as it swung closed behind her. Hopefully, by the time he reached twenty, she'd be back up on the sixth floor.

Hide-and-seek in a six-story office building. Sounded like a good way to kill some time.

Especially if she made sure she was naked by the time he found her.

10

AS MUCH AS LUCY WOULD have liked to stay in Ross's little house and learn everything there was to know about making love, she had to work on Christmas Eve. The photographer for whom she was interning had families coming in for holiday portraits and she needed to be there with bells on.

Literally. Jingle bells. They were attached to the curled-up toes of her silly elf shoes and she tinkled with every step.

One day, when she was a world-famous photographer, she'd laugh about this. But not now. It was just too ridiculous and embarrassing. So much for wanting to seem like a cool, collected, mature woman during her first-ever "morning after." Ross was going to look at her and think he'd spent the night with a teenager.

"Please tell me you'll wear that outfit tonight," Ross said, not attempting to hide his amusement when she emerged from the bathroom early Saturday morning.

"Ha ha."

"I mean it. You're totally hot. Hermie would never have left the North Pole to become a dentist if you were around."

"Dork."

"Elf." He grabbed her by the hips and pulled her close, laughing as her bobbing red feather poked him in the eye. He was still laughing when he pressed his mouth against hers for a deep, good morning kiss.

Lucy wobbled on her feet a little. Somehow, she suspected Ross's kiss—or even just the memory of his kiss—would *always* make her wobble.

"Are you ready?"

"Don't I look ready?" she said with a disgusted sigh. Then she added, "You're sure you don't mind driving me all the way back up to the city?"

"I told you, I have errands to run."

They'd spent time this morning wrapping and packing up his holiday gifts to his family. But she suspected there had to be shipping stores somewhere closer than Manhattan.

"I could take the train."

"Forget it," he said, ending the discussion.

The traffic heading into the city wasn't as bad as it would have been on a weekday. Most cars were heading out—obviously people who'd been stuck working right up until the twenty-third leaving for holiday weekends with family.

They reached the studio about a half hour early, and Lucy, who had a key, led him inside. "You really don't have to stay," she told him as she turned on the lights.

"I'm staying," he insisted, immediately stepping to a front window to glance back out at the street.

She knew why. Ross didn't trust Jude not to come here and harass her. Not that either of them really thought he'd try anything violent in broad daylight, while she was at work. But she wouldn't put it past him to come in and try to talk to her about why she should let last night's ugly incident go.

She wouldn't. In fact, this morning, with Ross's encouragement, she'd already called and spoken to someone at the police precinct near her apartment.

"Are you usually here alone in the mornings?" Ross asked, when, after ten minutes, nobody else had arrived.

"My boss is always late." Rolling her eyes, she added, "He's the irresponsible, creative genius type."

"So I see," he said as he followed her into the studio, where a holiday scene had been laid out. A large sleigh with velvet cushions stood in a corner, in front of a snowy backdrop. Surrounding it were mounds of white fluff that looked like snow. Woodland creatures, decorated trees, candy canes and icicles finished the scenario. "This is cute."

"Thanks," she said, pleased at the compliment, since she was the one who'd designed the whimsical scene. Her employer had never done more than drop a snowy screen behind a stool before she'd come onboard, and he'd already complimented her on the increased amount of traffic, telling her she had a knack for this kind of thing.

Funny, really, since she never intended to do it again. Surprisingly, though, as she stood looking at the results of her creativity, she felt a pang of sadness at the thought. She'd put a lot of effort into this and had actually enjoyed doing it.

Forget it. Paris fashion beats North Pole kiddieland any day.

Right. Definitely. Even if she did love hearing the squeals of delight of some of the littlest children who came in for holiday sittings, she would almost certainly love the squeals of millionaires as they eyed the latest fashions on the catwalk.

Hearing her cell phone ring, Lucy retrieved it, recognizing the studio owner's name. "Uh-oh," she mumbled, hoping this didn't mean the man would be later than usual.

A few seconds into the conversation, she realized it was worse than that. "You're not coming in today at *all?*"

"I'm sorry, it can't be helped! I fell last night and hurt my knee. I can't walk."

Huh. Considering the older man liked to dig into the spiked eggnog by noon, she had to wonder how he'd fallen.

"We only have a few appointments—you can handle them."

Lucy sputtered. She was an intern—an unpaid one at that. And he seriously wanted her to do his job, on Christmas Eve?

"I know this is going above and beyond," he said. "But I'd be so grateful. I will absolutely compensate you for your time."

She could just imagine what he'd consider fair compensation. Considering she had worked like a slave for three months without earning a penny, she'd be lucky to make a hundred bucks.

But hell, she was here. She was a photographer. And even if she didn't ever want to take the kinds of photographs he took, it was her chance to work professionally. So she agreed.

After she disconnected, and explained the situation, Ross offered to stay and help her. Lucy appreciated it, but knew he had things to do. Insisting that he go mail his packages, she added, "I'll check the book, but I think there are only appointments between ten and one. If you can get back by then and greet people as they come in, I'd really appreciate it."

Then she'd be finished for the day, and they could go do...whatever two lovers, who were strangers a day ago, one of whom didn't do Christmas, did on Christmas.

She could hardly wait.

"You're on," he promised as he headed toward the door. Before exiting, he said, "Keep this locked until ten, okay?"

She nodded. "I swear. Don't worry."

He gave her one of those devastating smiles that lit up his green eyes. "Can't help it, Lucy."

The way he said it, the warmth in his expression, made her smile for several minutes after he'd gone. But eventually, she had to set up for work.

Given the freedom to experiment, she decided to try out a few ideas, as long as the paying customers were willing. So by the time the first was scheduled to arrive, she'd already played around with some lighting effects, as well as a couple of her boss's specialty lenses.

Ross arrived back right on time, and with his help, she spent the next couple of hours enjoying the heck out of her job. For the first time, she wasn't just signing people in, collecting checks, selling overpriced packages, and trying to make cranky, wet little kids laugh, while nodding at every single idea her boss had. She was creating, trying new positions and lighting and special effects. She could feel the energy as she worked, and suspected these images would turn out to be something special.

By the time she'd finished with the last customer, it was after two. Ross had been a huge help, and once they were alone in the front office, she threw her arms around his neck and kissed him. "Thank you so much—what a fun day!"

"It was," he told her, laughing as he dropped his hands to her hips and squeezed her tighter. "You were fantastic. I don't know that I've ever seen anyone as great with kids as you are."

She rolled her eyes. "I wouldn't go that far."

"I would," he insisted. "You were really amazing. You should specialize in this."

"Fat chance," she snorted. "I have other plans. Big plans."

"Like?"

They began to clean up, getting ready to shut the studio down for the next few days. And while they did, Lucy told him about her upcoming study abroad trip. About her plans to photograph her way around the world. About the bright, exotic future she envisioned for herself, which had nothing to do with Santas or reindeer or chubby-cheeked infants.

He broke in with a few questions, but for the most part, just nodded, agreeing that her future sounded wonderful. But when all was said and done, he still murmured, "I still say you'd be great doing this, too."

"Not happening," she told him, knowing he didn't

truly understand. How could he? She hadn't come right out and told him that her need to escape to somewhere far away had a lot in common with her need to avoid Christmas and all the happy family trappings that came with it.

Lucy had loved photography from the time she was twelve and her parents had given her a "real" camera. She'd been the family photojournalist from that moment on, recording every event and capturing every wonderful smile.

But then the family and the smiles had disappeared. Their loss had been almost more than she could bear. So going out into the world and seeing exotic places and people through the lens of her camera sounded ideal to her, now that she could no longer see the people she'd always loved. Exciting, of course…but more, it sounded a lot less painful. Her heart wasn't going to be broken if a shot didn't land on the pages of a magazine. Not caring as much about her subjects was the smart choice, the right choice. The perfect way to live her life.

Ross's voice suddenly jolted her out of the moment of melancholy. "So, little girl, have you been good all year?"

Spinning around, she saw him sitting on the sleigh, patting his lap suggestively, like the world's sexiest Santa.

"Hmm," she said, sauntering over. "That depends on your definition of good."

He pulled her down on top of him. "After last night, you are my definition of good," he told her. "They should just put your picture on the G page in Webster's."

"Are you sure I'm not a little bit bad?"

He nuzzled her neck. "Only in the very best way."

Feeling soft and warm all over, she dropped her head back, inviting him further, loving the feel of his unshaven cheek against her skin. When he pressed his mouth to the hollow of her throat, she sighed. And when he moved lower, to tease the V-neck of her blouse, she leaned back even further. So far, she fell off his lap, onto a mountain of white, fluffy fake snow.

"Ow," she said, even as she laughed at herself.

He leaped off the seat and knelt beside her. "Are you okay?"

"I'm fine."

"You'd better let me check you all over and make sure you're not hurt."

Hearing the naughty tone, she feigned a deep sigh and sagged back into the fluff, which cushioned her like a giant feather bed. "Maybe you should. I do feel a little weak."

His eyes gleaming, Ross did as he'd threatened. Slowly, gently, he caressed her neck, brushed his thumbs over her collarbones, cupped her shoulders. As if he couldn't be certain using just his hands, he began kissing his way down her body as well. Every time she sighed, or flinched, he'd look up at her and ask, "Did that hurt?"

"Definitely not," she mumbled, rising up to meet his mouth.

He didn't tease her for long. Neither of them could stand that. As if he couldn't wait to be with her again—though it had only been hours since they'd left his bed—Ross unbuttoned her blouse, pulling it free of her flouncy skirt. He kissed his way to her breasts, bathing the sensitive tips through her bra.

"Mmm," she groaned, wrapping her fingers in his thick hair.

She loved that he was so into her breasts, loved the way he slipped the bra strap down and plumped each one with his hand before sucking deeply on her nipples. Each strong pull of his mouth sent a jolt of want through her body, and her tights felt even more restrictive than usual.

"Luce?" he mumbled as he pulled her skirt up around her waist and cupped her thigh.

"Hmm?"

"Since tomorrow's Christmas, does that mean you don't need this costume anymore?"

"I guess so," she murmured.

"Good."

He didn't explain what that meant, he simply showed her. Rising onto his knees, Ross reached for the crotch of her tights and carefully yanked. They tore open, exposing her sex completely, since she'd been wearing nothing underneath.

"Good God," he muttered, sitting back on his heels to look at her.

Seeing that shocked delight in his face gave her such a feeling of feminine power. She deliberately spread her legs, revealing more of herself, loving the way his hand shook as he lifted it to rub his jaw.

It wasn't shaking when he reached out to touch her, though. She hissed as his long, warm fingers stroked her, delving into the slick crevice between her thighs. She was wet and ready, wanting him desperately.

Fortunately, Ross had brought a condom, and she

laid back in the fluff, watching him push his jeans out of the way and don the protection. She lifted a leg invitingly, knowing he'd like the feel of the silky fabric of the tights against his bare hip.

She imagined he'd like it in other places, too. But his hips and that amazingly tight male butt were a good start. Without a word, she pulled him down to her, inviting him into her warmth.

She was still new enough at this to gasp when he entered her, but Ross kissed away the sound. His warm tongue made love to her mouth as he pressed further into her body, until they were fully joined. Lucy wrapped her legs around him and rolled her hips up in welcome.

He lengthened his strokes, filling and stretching and pleasing her so much she cried out at how good it felt. He was so thick and hard inside her, and she was used to this enough to want him harder, faster. Deeper.

"More," she demanded. "You're being so careful... you can stop. I want it all, Ross. Give it to me."

He groaned. Then, as if he'd just been awaiting the invitation, pulled out and slammed back into her. Hard, deep. Unbelievably good.

"Oh, yeah. More."

"You're sure."

"Absolutely," she insisted. "Give me everything you've got."

He didn't reply with words. Instead, to her surprise, Ross pulled out of her and reached for her hips. His face a study in need and hunger, he rolled her over onto her tummy, then wrapped an arm around her waist and pulled her up onto her knees. Lucy shivered, more excited than she'd ever been in her life.

She was wet and hot and ready, and when he thrust into her from behind, she threw her head back and screamed a little.

Still buried deep inside her, he grabbed her tights again. It took just one more tug and he'd ripped them completely in half from waist to thigh, baring her bottom entirely. Filling his hands with her hips, he drove into her again. Heat to heat, skin to skin.

Lucy just about lost her mind. She loved it sweet and slow and tender. But oh, did she ever love it hot and wild and *wicked*. In fact, she realized, she loved each and every thing Ross Marshall did to her.

Especially that. And, oh, *that*.

They strained and writhed, gave and took, and soon, a stunning orgasm tore through her. As if he'd just been waiting for her to reach that point, Ross immediately buried his face in her hair, kept his arms wrapped tightly around her waist and let himself go over the edge, too.

They collapsed together on the fluff. He rolled onto his side, tugging her with him, spooning her from behind. Lucy had a hard time catching her breath, but oh, God, was it worth it.

Finally, when their breathing had calmed down a bit, Ross said, "So, since you're finished with work, was that the official start of the holiday?"

"If so," she said, sounding vehement, "then merry Christmas to us!"

He hugged her closer. "And to us a good night."

THEY HAD A HELL OF A good night. An amazing night, as far as Ross was concerned.

After he and Lucy had cleaned up the studio and

left, they hadn't headed right back for Brooklyn. Instead they'd tooled around the city a little bit. He'd even managed to convince her to go up to Rockefeller Center and go ice skating. Sure, they'd been blade-to-blade with a thousand other people who had the same idea, but it was worth it.

They'd walked past every decorated window on Park and Fifth Avenues, had gone down as far as Macy's and jostled a place in line to see those, too. Lucy grumbled a lot, but beneath the complaints he'd heard something that tugged at his heart. A sweetness, an excitement, a longing she hadn't verbalized, but was there all the same.

Underneath it all—the vibrant, gonna-go-see-the-world, and I-don't-care-about-Christmas veneer—was a pretty innocent twenty-two-year-old. One who had lost her anchor at a young age and didn't trust the world not to slam her again. Hard.

He wouldn't have admitted it, but Ross really liked trying to get Lucy to enjoy the holiday season, despite her own best efforts to dislike it. And while he wasn't totally certain she'd like the gift he'd bought her before going back to help at the studio this morning, he hoped she at least understood the intentions behind it.

"That was great," he said as he set his fork onto his empty plate. They'd just finished dinner at his tiny kitchen table.

Lucy had insisted on cooking for him, though she'd warned him she wasn't up to anything fancy. Still, it had been the first real "home-cooked" meal he'd had in ages, and he didn't think meatloaf had ever tasted so good.

He stood to clear the table and clean up the kitchen.

"Let me help you," she said, starting to rise.

"You cooked," he told her. "Go sit down and relax for a while. I've got this."

"You're sure?"

"Of course." It struck him, suddenly, how domestic the whole thing was. Which was pretty bizarre, considering they'd known each other for a day and a half.

The best day and a half ever.

That was a crazy realization, but it was true nonetheless. He couldn't remember a better time than he'd had since meeting Lucy Fleming. Honestly, wondering what was going to happen next had him more excited than anything in a very long time.

Cleaning the kitchen quickly, he went into the other room, and found Lucy sitting on the sofa, with her head back and her eyes closed. She'd turned on the stereo and Christmas music played softly in the background. He was about to open his mouth to tease her about breaking her own rule when he saw the teardrop on her cheek.

Saying nothing, he joined her on the couch, tugging her against him so that her head rested on his shoulder. They sat there for a long time in silence, listening to the music, watching the way the silly camera flash—now covered with a green sheet of plastic—cast glimmers of light on the Christmas tree.

Finally, she shifted in his arms and looked up at him. "This is the nicest Christmas Eve I've had in a very long time."

"I'm glad. Not *too* traditional for you?"

"No. It's perfect." She licked her lips. "I know you're very close to your family, and this is all probably hard for you to understand…"

"I can understand it with my brain," he told her, meaning it. "But my heart doesn't even want to try to understand. I just can't imagine what it must be like."

His father drove him crazy, but Ross still loved him, and his mother. He couldn't even fathom having his world yanked out from under him like Lucy had, couldn't comprehend getting a phone call telling you the people you'd always assumed would be there were suddenly gone.

People expected to outlive their parents, that was natural. But not until they reached at least middle age. Not until their own kids had gotten a chance to meet their grandparents. His own parents were pretty young, only in their early mid-fifties, and Ross fully expected another twenty to thirty years of arguing with his Dad and being fussed over by his Mom. He wouldn't have it any other way.

"I can tell you what it's like," she said. "It's like waking up one day and realizing someone's torn half your heart out of your chest. Your life is no longer about the number of years you've lived, or the ones you have in front of you. It becomes measured by before and after that one moment."

He understood. It broke his heart, but he definitely understood. He hugged her close, smoothing her hair, kissing her temple.

"But then," she whispered, "the hole starts to fill in. You remember the good times from before that moment, and also start to acknowledge the good ones that come after." She shifted on the couch, looking up at him. Her beautiful brown eyes were luminous, but no more tears marred her cheeks. As if she wanted him to see that she was melancholy, but not heartbroken. "This weekend, you've given me good moments, Ross. And I'll never forget them."

He bent to her, brushing his mouth across hers in a tender kiss. She kissed him back, sweetly, gently, then smiled up at him.

"So," he said, knowing the time was right, "is it okay if I give you your Christmas present now?"

She eyed him warily.

"It's not much," he told her as he got up and went to the tree. He'd hidden the wrapped package behind it when they'd arrived home earlier this evening.

"You shouldn't have gotten me anything," she insisted. "I don't have anything for you."

He winked and raised a flirtatious brow. "I'm sure I'll think of something you can give me later."

"Hmm…why don't we see what's in here, then I'll decide just what you deserve to get in return." She took the present, and though a shadow of trepidation crossed her face, and she nibbled her lip lightly, he would also swear he saw a glimmer of a smile.

He sat on the opposite end of the couch, watching her unwrap the box. As she opened the lid, and stared down in silence at the gift inside, he couldn't help wondering if he'd made a mistake.

Maybe it was too soon. Maybe she wasn't ready. Maybe she'd think he didn't understand, after all.

She reached in and pulled out the snow globe, shaking it gently, watching the white glitter swirl around the scene inside.

It wasn't anything funny, like her brother would give her, and certainly wasn't intended to replace the peace sign Santa that had been broken. Instead it was simple, pretty—traditional. A house with a snowy roof and a wreath on the door. Warm, yellow light coming from the windows, where a family could be imagined to have gathered. A car parked outside. A tree-studded landscape. It portrayed a quiet Christmas night, when all was calm and bright.

"I just thought, since your other one was broken…"

"It's beautiful," she whispered. "Absolutely beautiful."

She twisted the knob on the bottom, and Deck The Halls began to play. Smiling, Lucy carefully set the globe down on the table. "Thank you."

"You're welcome, Lucy."

The song on the radio ended, and an announcer came on to mention the time—midnight on the nose.

They looked at the tree, then at each other. With no more sign of those tears, Lucy whispered, "Merry Christmas, Ross."

She rose from the couch and extended her hand. Ross took it and together they walked to his bedroom. They exchanged langorous, intimate kisses as they slowly undressed. Throughout the long night hours, they didn't have sex, they made love. He had never been sure of the distinction before, but now, he finally got it.

He fell asleep with a smile on his face, and was pretty sure it stayed there all night long. Because he was still smiling hours later, on Christmas morning, when he woke up to a naked Lucy wrapped in his arms…and a ringing phone.

"What time is it?" she asked in a sleep-filled voice.

He glanced at the clock. "Only six-thirty."

There would only be one person calling this early. His kid sister was always the first one up on Christmas, and she'd probably already checked her email and seen the cyber gift card he'd ordered for her.

Checking the caller ID on his phone, and seeing his parents' phone number, he chuckled and opened it, fully expecting to hear his sister's joy-filled, chattery voice.

"Hello?"

A pause. A sob.

Then the bottom fell out of his entire world.

11

LUCY WOKE UP CHRISTMAS morning feeling nice, warm and toasty. That wasn't just because of the incredibly hot, sexy, naked man against whom she was lying, but also because the heating vent right above the foldout was blowing out a steady stream of warm air.

The power was on. *Hallelujah.*

She lay there for a few minutes, relieved, but also a tiny bit sad. Power was good. Great, in fact. But it signaled something: a return to normalcy. The real world was knocking at the doors of their romantic little love nest, reminding them it was really a six story office building in Chicago.

For thirty-six hours, they'd been able to pretend the rest of the world didn't exist. Now that they were wired again, however, they were just a phone call away from everyone.

She should make use of that and call Sam, who might be worried. Hopefully he had been too busy to try to reach her. But at the very least she needed to call and wish him a merry Christmas…or at least a *bah, humbug.*

She wondered if it would be merry for her. Before yesterday, she would have laughed at the idea. Now, though, she honestly wasn't sure.

It would probably be smart to cut her losses, grab the memory of the gift she'd already received this holiday season, and get out while the getting was good. She and Ross had shared a magical Christmas Eve—for the second time in her life. But they'd already proved once that they couldn't last much beyond that. So what kind of fool would she be to let him back into her heart again, the way she'd let him back into her arms?

Anybody could make a lovely, romantic memory out of the holiday season and some snow. They'd never had to try to exist out in the real world.

And maybe they shouldn't. Maybe they weren't meant to.

Saddened by that thought, she slowly sat up and stretched. She peered over Ross's shoulder toward the wall of windows and realized that not only had the snow stopped, but the sky was trying to be all blue and sunny. There was also a distinct sound of some kind of motor nearby.

Curious, she climbed out of bed and went to the window, which overlooked the parking lot. To her surprise, it was already half-cleared. A truck with a plow was working on the lot, and a small skid loader was taking care of the mounds of snow on the walkways.

"Damn," she whispered. Not only were they now connected electronically with the world, it looked like their "snowed-in" status was about to change, too. Their private holiday adventure had come to an end.

"Merry Christmas," he said from the bed, his voice thick with sleep.

Though she wanted to respond in kind, the words stuck a little in her throat, which had thickened with every second since she'd awoken. "Good morning."

"Does it feel warmer in here, or is it just because I'm staring at you and you're naked?"

She laughed softly and returned to the bed, bending to kiss him as she crawled in beside him. "Power's on. And the parking lot's almost cleared."

He frowned. "Remind me to fire that snow clearing company."

Ross didn't sound any happier about being "rescued" than she felt. Maybe because, like her, he wasn't sure what was going to happen when they returned to reality.

Did they have what it took to go beyond this weekend? To actually work in a day-to-day relationship? With his ties to his family and this business and this city…and her sometimes whimsical need to change direction and explore new opportunities, were they really cut out to be together?

She had no idea. Nor did she really want to talk to him about it yet. She had some thinking to do. And it would probably be best to do it alone.

"I guess you ought to call your family and let them know you're okay," she said. "They've probably been very worried."

He nodded. "Listen, why don't you come with…"

She knew what he was going to ask and held a hand up, palm out. "Thanks, but no thanks."

"I'm sure they'd love to meet you."

"Bah humbug, remember?"

"Lucy…"

"Please don't," she said as she got up and reached for her clothes and began pulling them on. As much as she'd like to stay naked in bed with Ross, she knew things had changed. She felt a lot less free and a lot more worried than she had last night. The presence of the rest of the world in their strange relationship had thrown her off-kilter. Where a few hours ago she had been filled with nothing but contentment and satisfaction, now the only things that filled her head were questions and concerns.

"I need some time," she told him. "I'd really just like to go home and take a shower."

"What about Christmas dinner?"

Turkey subs out of the break room had sounded just about perfect. Going with him to his parents' estate for a grand meal with a big family? Not so much.

"Please don't push it," she said, hearing the edge in her voice and getting mad at herself. He was trying to share something special—his family's holiday.

"Okay," he said. "I understand."

Since she didn't understand herself, she doubted that, but didn't want to argue with him. Not after the wonderful day they'd had yesterday and the beautiful, amazing, incredible nights in that narrow foldout bed.

"You can use the phone on my desk if you want to call Sam," he told her. "If the power's on, the lines should be working. Just dial 9 first."

Thanking him, she finished dressing and went to the desk. She got Sam's voice mail and left him a message. She checked her cell phone—still no reception—and decided to call her home phone and see if there were any messages.

She dialed home, then entered the security code. When she heard she had two messages from Friday, she winced, realizing she'd never even listened to them when she got home the other night. She'd been too busy masturbating in the bathtub while thinking of Ross.

A voice she didn't recognize came on the line. "Ms. Fleming, this is Janet Sturgeon, I'm with *Parents Place* magazine. I'm sorry for calling right before the holidays, but we really wanted to reach you. Everyone in the office just loved your photo essay."

She sent up a mental cheer. But the voice wasn't finished.

"And of course we all remember the great work you've done for us in the past. Anyway, we're making some changes here at headquarters and were wondering if you might be interested in coming to New York to discuss a more permanent working position with us? We're looking for an artistic director. We all really like what you do and think you would be a great fit with our staff."

Lucy's jaw had slowly become unhinged while she listened. She'd been hoping for a *Yes, we'll take your work and pay you X dollars.* But a job offer? At least, the offer of an interview for a job? She'd never imagined it.

Well, that was a lie, of course she'd imagined it. She'd thought many times about getting out of the self-employment wading pool and into the bigger publishing ocean. And *Parents Place* was a huge part of that ocean. The chance to work for them, to be an artistic director for a major national publication...honestly, it was like someone had just handed her the winning prize for a lottery, when she'd never bought a ticket.

Her mind had drifted off, and she'd missed the phone number the caller had left at the end. Lucy saved the message to listen to again when she got home and thought about what to say when she called the woman back tomorrow.

"Lucy? Are you okay?"

Ross was watching her from the alcove. He'd finished dressing, and swept a hand through his thick, sleep-tousled hair, looking perfect and sexy and gorgeous. Her heart somersaulted in her chest, as it always did when she looked at the man in broad daylight. Or, hell, in pitch darkness.

Only now, there was a faint squeezing sensation in her heart as well.

Don't be silly, you don't even know if you'd actually get the job yet. Or if you'd take it.

True. She couldn't let herself get upset about what could possibly happen in the future, and what it meant for her and Ross. For all she knew, there was no her and Ross. This weekend had been amazing and wonderful...but she had already acknowledged there might not be more than that.

There won't be if you're in New York.

Which made her wonder—would he care if she left? Would he ask her not to go?

"Lucy? Is everything okay? Was it Sam?"

She shook her head slowly and lowered the receiver back onto the cradle. Trying to keep her voice steady, so she wouldn't reveal either her excitement, or her incredible turmoil over what this could mean for them, she told him about the phone call.

Ross didn't react right away. He didn't immediately smile and congratulate her. Neither did he frown and insist that she couldn't possibly think about leaving now, when so much between them was up in the air.

So maybe it's not. Maybe everything was settled in that bed in the past thirty-six hours, and it's all over and we are both supposed to just go merrily on with our lives.

God, did she not want to believe that. But it was possible. To Ross, this may have just been a one-time thing. Maybe he couldn't care less if she went. She just didn't know. And honestly, she wasn't sure how to ask.

"I see. Well, that's exciting," he finally said.

"It could be," she replied carefully.

"When would you go back to New York?"

Yell, damn it. Show some kind of emotion.

"She said they wanted to interview me immediately, this week if possible."

"I don't imagine the airports are going to be open for a day or two. Maybe by late Tuesday, or Wednesday."

"Maybe," she said, wondering how he could be so calm, why he wouldn't reveal a thing about what he was thinking.

Why he wasn't telling her he didn't want her to go.

But he didn't. Instead, still calm and reasonable, as if they'd just finished a dinner date rather than a thirty-six hour, emotionally-charged sexual marathon, he helped her straighten up the office and the break room, hiding evidence of the wild weekend idyll that had taken place there. Everything went back in its spot, the borrowed coats returned, the food neatly put away. Even the foldout was made and folded up. No evidence that they'd been here at all.

The realization made her incredibly sad. But there was nothing she could do about it.

Finally, with nothing left to do, they dressed in warm clothes, and headed downstairs. They had no problem getting out to the parking lot, and Ross paid his contractor a little extra to dig out their cars. So, by twelve noon, they were ready to go, neither too concerned about their drive, considering the plows and salt trucks had been out in force most of the night.

Chicago was a city that was used to dealing with snow. Despite the wicked Christmas Eve blizzard, things would likely get back to normal pretty easily. If anything was ever normal again. Right now, Lucy wasn't sure about the definition of that word.

"You sure you're okay to drive home?" he asked.

She nodded. "I'll be fine, it's only a couple of miles."

He opened her car door for her. It was warm inside; she'd let it idle for a few minutes while they stood outside saying goodbye. Or, not saying goodbye. So far, they'd said anything but.

She wasn't sure what she was waiting for him to say. Or if he was waiting, too. Or what either of them could say that would make this all right, make them both understand where they'd been and where they were going.

In the end, they didn't say much of anything. Ross simply leaned down and brushed his mouth across hers, their breath mingling in the icy air. Then he whispered, "Merry Christmas, Lucy."

She managed a tremulous smile and nodded.

"Bye, Ross."

Her heart was screaming at her to say something else. Her brain was, too. But she couldn't find the words, didn't know what he wanted to hear.

So she simply got in her car, watched him get into his, and then they both drove away.

AFTER GOING HOME TO CHANGE and shower, and call the hospital to check on Chip—who was going to be all right—Ross headed out to his parents' place. His family had been holding their celebration until he got there. So he tried to pretend he gave a damn about the holiday and wasn't utterly miserable.

He didn't think he succeeded. His smile was tight, his laughter fake and the strain had to be visible. He couldn't keep his mind on the games, got lost in the middle of conversations and generally walked around in a daze for most of the afternoon.

All he could think about was Lucy. The time they'd spent together…and the way they'd parted.

He just couldn't understand it, couldn't begin to comprehend how she could have spent the weekend with him, doing everything they'd done, saying everything they'd said, then casually talk about moving back to New York. It made no sense.

He would have bet his last dollar that she loved him, that she'd always loved him, as he'd always loved her. But the words had never come out of her mouth, not even when he'd told her how he'd felt about her all those years ago.

You're the one who left her. You did the heartbreaking, a voice in his head reminded him. So maybe it wasn't so surprising that she wasn't going to just rush right back into this.

But to rush to the east coast instead? What sense did that make?

"So, are you going to tell us who she is?"

Ross jerked his head up when his kid sister Annie—who was no longer a little kid, but instead a college junior—entered the room. "Excuse me?"

"Come on, everybody can tell you've got woman troubles. We haven't seen you this mopey about a girl since you moved back home from New York after losing that girl…Linda?"

"Lucy. Her name is Lucy," he muttered, looking away and frowning.

Hearing Annie's surprised gasp, he wished he hadn't said a word. "Wait, are we talking about Lucy now?"

"What makes you ask that?"

"Well, you said her name *is* Lucy. Plus, the way you say her name, bro. It's like going back in time six years. I remember exactly how you were when you first got back after Dad got sick. I've never seen you so hung up on anyone."

There was a good reason for that. He'd never *been* so hung up on anyone else.

"So what's the story? Why didn't you invite her over for Christmas dinner?"

"I did. She…doesn't really like Christmas." He didn't want to share any details of Lucy's private life, but did explain, "She has some pretty bad memories of this time of year."

"So where is she? Is she here in Chicago?"

"Yes, she moved here. She's home at her apartment now."

"Dude! Harsh!"

He rolled his eyes, still not used to hearing his sister talk like an eighteen-year-old guy, which seemed to be how all young women talked now.

"You left her sitting at home, alone in her apartment, on Christmas?"

"Like I said, I asked her to come here. She wanted to go home. Alone."

Annie's eyebrows wagged, which was when he realized he'd slipped up. Again. "*Go* home, huh? As in, she was with you for the past couple of days during your big trapped-in-the-snow emergency?"

"Shut up," he muttered.

She laughed. "Look, all I gotta say is, if I was seeing someone, and he left me sitting at home all alone on Christmas, I'd feel absolutely sure he didn't give a damn about me."

"You're not Lucy," he muttered.

"Good thing for you," she said, getting up and sauntering toward the door. "Because if I were, I'd have said later, dude, and made you think I didn't care any more about you than you did about me."

She left the room, leaving Ross sitting there alone. But his sibling's words remained. In fact, they somehow seemed to get louder…and louder.

He knew Lucy wasn't the type to play games. But he also knew she had to be feeling very unsure about them—about him—right now. Considering he'd walked out on her Christmas Day six years ago and had stopped calling her shortly thereafter, why wouldn't she have doubts? Why wouldn't she have questions?

Why wouldn't she expect that he wouldn't give a damn if she decided to move back to New York?

In trying to be calm and rational and fair, had he made her think he didn't care? Had hiding his fear of losing her again made it that much more likely to happen?

No. That just wouldn't do. No way was he going to let her think he didn't want her. Lucy might want to leave, she might view this great career move as the next logical step in her life. But he wasn't going to let her make that decision without making sure she knew how he felt.

Which meant he needed to go talk to her. And this time, there would be nothing left unsaid.

OF ALL THE sucky Christmases Lucy had ever experienced in her life, this one had to rank right up there among the suckiest.

Oh, it had started off great. Magically, in fact. She'd awakened this morning in the arms of an amazing man, sure she'd never been happier in her life.

But since she'd arrived home—alone—and moped around her apartment—alone—and eaten a frozen dinner—alone—Lucy couldn't find a single positive thing about it.

She'd tried doing her online shopping—boring. She'd cleaned her apartment—more boring. She'd answered a few emails, checked her appointment book, looked into flights to New York.

Boring. Boring.

And heartbreaking.

Heartbreaking, because she didn't want to fly to New York. Not under these circumstances, anyway. Not without knowing how Ross felt about it—whether he gave a damn.

This morning, when she'd first heard the message about the potential job offer, oh, it had been exciting, a great validation. Thinking that a major magazine was seeking her out for her talent was a huge ego boost and a true reinforcement that she'd made the right choice when switching gears in her career.

But she didn't particularly want to move back to New York. She liked Chicago. She liked living near her brother again. She liked the people she'd met and the studio she'd rented and the life she was living.

Most of all, she liked being near the man she loved.

"Hell," she whispered that evening as she sat on her couch, listening to Christmas music on an internet radio station.

She loved him. She loved Ross Marshall. She always had. He'd entered her heart six years ago and had never left it, despite time and distance and other relationships.

Some people could fall in and out of love. Some loved only once in a lifetime. She suspected she was one of those people. Which would be wonderful, if only she didn't love a guy who didn't seem to care if she moved a thousand miles away.

Feeling truly sorry for herself, she almost didn't hear the knock. At first, she assumed her neighbors' kids were banging around with all their new Christmas toys. They'd been filled with joy and laughter all day, and she'd smiled at the sounds coming through the thin walls. But the sound came again, and she realized someone was at her door.

She glanced at the clock, seeing it was after eight. She'd finally reached Sam this afternoon, and he'd told her he was working all night again. But perhaps he'd managed to swing by on a break or something.

She went to the door and opened it with a smile. The smile faded when she saw not her brother, but someone she'd never expected to see at her doorstep tonight.

"Ross?"

"Can I come in?"

Stunned, not only because he'd told her he was going out to his family's, but also because, as far as she knew, he'd had no idea where she lived, she stepped aside and beckoned him in. "How did you…"

"Stella. She had both your work and your home addresses in her BlackBerry."

"Is everything all right? Your family?"

"Fine. By now they're probably engaged in the annual Trivial Pursuit Christmas marathon."

Still unsure why he'd come, and not knowing what to say, she quickly asked, "And your security guard?"

"He's going to pull through," he said.

"I'm so glad." Twisting her hands together, she finally remembered her manners. "Can I take your coat? Would you like to sit down?"

He took off his coat, but didn't sit in the chair to which she gestured. Instead, sounding and looking somber, he stared into her eyes and said, "If I ask you a question, will you answer me truthfully?"

"Of course."

"Okay." Stepping closer, close enough that she smelled his spicy cologne and felt his body's warmth, he asked, "Do you want to move back to New York?"

Talk about putting her on the spot. She crossed her arms over her chest, rubbing her hands up and down them and thought about her answer. Her first instinct was to answer his question with a question—*do you want me to stay?*

But they'd played enough games, lost enough time dancing around the truth or making decisions for each other without benefit of a real, genuine conversation.

So she would be nothing but honest, both with him, and with herself.

"No. I don't."

He closed his eyes and sighed, so visibly relieved, she almost smiled.

"My turn to ask you a question," she countered.

"Okay."

Drawing a deep breath, and hoping her voice wouldn't quiver, she asked, "Do you want me to stay?"

He didn't hesitate, not even for an instant. "Oh, *hell* yes."

Though pleased by his vehemence, she tilted her head in confusion. "Then why did you act like you didn't care earlier?"

"Why did you let me think you wanted to go?"

Neither answered for a second…then they both replied in unison. "Because we're idiots."

Laughter bubbled between them, then Ross stepped closer, dropping his hands to her hips and tugging her to him. She lifted hers to his shoulders and looked up at him, seeing the warmth and the tenderness in his green eyes. Even without the words being said, she knew what he was thinking, what he was feeling. What his heart was telling him.

Because her heart was telling her the same thing.

They were meant to be together. They always had been. Time and circumstance had separated them, yes. But, maybe that was how it had to be. They'd been young and impulsive. And she hadn't truly been ready to accept love and happiness, to offer the kind of trusting, loving relationship Ross deserved.

Now she was ready. And they'd found their way back to each other. It had taken years, and moving to another city, but their lives had come full circle and this week, they'd recreated the past.

Only, this time, it would end differently. They weren't going to let anything come between them.

This time, they would make it work.

"I love you," he said, and her heart sang.

He lifted a hand to cup her face. "I let you go once. I wasn't about to make the same mistake again."

"What if I had said I wanted to go to New York?"

"I would have said fine, when do we leave?"

She started to smile, at least until she saw he meant it. Then she could only stare at him in shock. "Are you serious?"

"Very serious."

"But how—"

"I talked to my father when I was out at the house today. I told him I had let you get away once, but it wasn't going to happen again. And that while I'd like to stay at Elite, if it came down to it, I was going to do what was right for *me* for a change. Live my life for myself, since I've been living it for everyone else for the past six years."

"How did he react?"

He looked away. "I think that's the closest I've ever seen my father to tears."

She sucked in a breath.

"Not because he was upset, but because he finally had the chance to tell me how damned grateful he is for everything I've done, and how much he wants me to be happy." Ross shook his head slowly. "To tell you the truth, I couldn't believe it. He's never said anything like that to me before."

Knowing how much that had to have meant to him,

Lucy rose on tiptoe and brushed her mouth against his. "I'm so glad."

"Me, too."

"But your father doesn't have anything to worry about, and neither do your shareholders."

"We can go if you want to," he insisted.

"I don't," she insisted back, being completely honest. "I'm finished running off to do new things, in new places, just to avoid having to ever expose myself to pain and hurt again. There's no love without risk…but there's no life without love."

Then, realizing she had never actually said it, she gave him the most honest, genuine present she could think to give him. "I love you, Ross. I always have, I always will."

He smiled tenderly, then bent to kiss her, slowly, lovingly. And having those words on their lips made it taste that much sweeter, made it mean that much more.

When they finally ended the kiss, they remained locked in each other's arms, swaying slowly to the holiday music playing softly in the background. "Joy to the World."

How fitting. For the first time in what seemed like forever, her life felt filled to the brim with joy. Because Ross was in it. And she knew, deep down to her very soul, that he always would be.

"Merry Christmas, Lucy," he whispered against her cheek.

"Merry Christmas, Ross."

She tightened her arms around him, wanting to capture this feeling and imprint it in her mind forever, like a beautiful photograph. The first moment of the rest of their lives.

There would be many more, she knew. Some beautiful, probably some sad.

But no matter what, they would all be filled with love.

Epilogue

Two Years Later

CURLED UP TOGETHER on the sofa, Lucy and Ross watched out their front window as the first flakes of Christmas snow began to fall. The weatherman wasn't predicting a major storm—nothing like the one that had trapped them in Ross's office building two years earlier—aka the best blizzard of all time. No, this was quiet and sweet, a nighttime snow as gentle and peaceful as the carols playing softly on the stereo behind them.

Wrapped in the arms of the man she loved, here inside the beautiful home they'd finished building together and had moved into last spring, Lucy didn't mind if it snowed all night. She had everything—and everyone—she needed, right here within these walls.

"Here it comes," he murmured, tightening his arms around her.

"Mmm-hmm."

They remained silent for a moment, watching the white flakes drift down, slowly at first, then more steadily. Lucy suddenly realized, looking out that huge front window that overlooked the water, that this must be what it was like to be inside a snow globe. Perhaps the very one Ross had given her all those years ago, which now had a place of honor on the center of the mantelpiece. She was tucked inside that happy home, with the warm yellow light in the window and the cars in the driveway and the snowy evergreens all around.

She smiled, loving the image, thinking back to that Christmas Eve. What, she wondered, would that girl, that twenty-two-year-old Lucy, have thought if she could have foreseen this future? She probably wouldn't have believed it, and it would have scared her to death. But, deep down she knew she would have been very hopeful—because that day had opened her eyes to a world of possibilities.

All because of the man holding her so tenderly, humming Silent Night as he kissed her temple.

She looked up at him, so handsome in the glow from the fire, and whispered, "Merry Christmas, Ross."

He smiled back and brushed his lips against hers. "Merry Christmas, wife."

No more *bah humbug* for Lucy. No more building walls against things like memories, and holidays…and love. That part of her life was over.

Ross stretched a little and chuckled. "Am I rotten for being glad my parents and your brother decided to stay home and come over tomorrow, after they see how much snow falls?"

She laughed softly, understanding him so well. "Not unless I'm rotten, too, because I feel the same way."

It wasn't that either of them begrudged the visit—

she actually adored his family, and her brother's new girlfriend. They certainly had plenty of room for everyone in the huge house. But she couldn't deny being happy things had worked out this way. Now they would have tonight and tomorrow morning for themselves, getting a start on creating holiday memories and traditions of their own.

She was ready for that. Ready to incorporate the ghosts of her Christmases past into her present and her future. Ready to open her heart to the magical season of giving that she'd once loved so very much…and move forward, molding it, changing it, shaping it into something that was just hers, and Ross's, and their family's.

"It's not that I don't love them…"

"It's just because tomorrow's so special," she replied.

Very special. Not just because it was their first holiday season in their new home. Not just because it was the first Christmas since they'd gotten married last year, on Christmas Day. Not just because they were still wildly in love and so incredibly happy. Not even because Lucy had become a fan of Christmas again.

No, they were glad to be alone because they both wanted to savor and rejoice in the early present they'd received ten days ago. Well, two presents.

They were sleeping upstairs in matching cribs, one with a blue baby blanket, the other pink. Scott and Jennifer—Jenny—named after the grandparents they would never know.

When Ross had suggested the names, she'd thought her heart would break. Not with sadness, but because of how happy her parents would be to see her so deeply loved by such an amazing man.

That, she knew, was the greatest Christmas gift she would ever receive. And she'd be getting that gift every day for the rest of her life.

* * * * *

PASSION

For a spicier, decidedly hotter read—
this is your destination for romance!

COMING NEXT MONTH
AVAILABLE DECEMBER 27, 2011

#657 THE PHOENIX
Men Out of Uniform
Rhonda Nelson

#658 BORN READY
Uniformly Hot!
Lori Wilde

#659 STRAIGHT TO THE HEART
Forbidden Fantasies
Samantha Hunter

#660 SEX, LIES AND MIDNIGHT
Undercover Operatives
Tawny Weber

#661 BORROWING A BACHELOR
All the Groom's Men
Karen Kendall

#662 THE PLAYER'S CLUB: SCOTT
The Player's Club
Cathy Yardley

REQUEST YOUR FREE BOOKS!
2 FREE NOVELS PLUS 2 FREE GIFTS!

red-hot reads!

YES! Please send me 2 FREE Harlequin® Blaze™ novels and my 2 FREE gifts (gifts are worth about $10). After receiving them, if I don't wish to receive any more books, I can return the shipping statement marked "cancel." If I don't cancel, I will receive 6 brand-new novels every month and be billed just $4.49 per book in the U.S. or $4.96 per book in Canada. That's a saving of at least 14% off the cover price. It's quite a bargain. Shipping and handling is just 50¢ per book in the U.S. and 75¢ per book in Canada.* I understand that accepting the 2 free books and gifts places me under no obligation to buy anything. I can always return a shipment and cancel at any time. Even if I never buy another book, the two free books and gifts are mine to keep forever.

151/351 HDN FEQE

Name _____ (PLEASE PRINT) _____

Address _____ Apt. # _____

City _____ State/Prov. _____ Zip/Postal Code _____

Signature (if under 18, a parent or guardian must sign)

Mail to the **Reader Service:**
IN U.S.A.: P.O. Box 1867, Buffalo, NY 14240-1867
IN CANADA: P.O. Box 609, Fort Erie, Ontario L2A 5X3

Not valid for current subscribers to Harlequin Blaze books.

Want to try two free books from another line?
Call 1-800-873-8635 or visit www.ReaderService.com.

* Terms and prices subject to change without notice. Prices do not include applicable taxes. Sales tax applicable in N.Y. Canadian residents will be charged applicable taxes. Offer not valid in Quebec. This offer is limited to one order per household. All orders subject to credit approval. Credit or debit balances in a customer's account(s) may be offset by any other outstanding balance owed by or to the customer. Please allow 4 to 6 weeks for delivery. Offer available while quantities last.

Your Privacy—The Reader Service is committed to protecting your privacy. Our Privacy Policy is available online at www.ReaderService.com or upon request from the Reader Service.

We make a portion of our mailing list available to reputable third parties that offer products we believe may interest you. If you prefer that we not exchange your name with third parties, or if you wish to clarify or modify your communication preferences, please visit us at www.ReaderService.com/consumerschoice or write to us at Reader Service Preference Service, P.O. Box 9062, Buffalo, NY 14269. Include your complete name and address.

HB11B

Harlequin® *Desire*

ALWAYS POWERFUL, PASSIONATE AND PROVOCATIVE.

USA TODAY BESTSELLING AUTHOR

KATHIE DeNOSKY

BRINGS YOU ANOTHER STORY FROM

TEXAS CATTLEMAN'S CLUB: THE SHOWDOWN

Childhood rivals Brad Price and Abigail Langley have found themselves once again in competition, this time for President of the Texas Cattleman's Club. But when Brad's plans are interrupted when his baby niece is suddenly placed under his care, he finds himself asking Abigail for help. As Election Day draws near, will Brad still be going after the Presidency or Abigail's heart? Find out in:

IN BED WITH THE OPPOSITION

Available December wherever books are sold.

*Brittany Grayson survived a horrible ordeal at the hands
of a serial killer known as The Professional...
who's after her now?*

*Harlequin® Romantic Suspense presents a new installment
in Carla Cassidy's reader-favorite miniseries,*
LAWMEN OF BLACK ROCK.

Enjoy a sneak peek of
TOOL BELT DEFENDER.

*Available January 2012
from Harlequin® Romantic Suspense.*

"**B**rittany?" His voice was deep and pleasant and made
her realize she'd been staring at him openmouthed through
the screen door.

"Yes, I'm Brittany and you must be..." Her mind suddenly went blank.

"Alex. Alex Crawford, Chad's friend. You called him
about a deck?"

As she unlocked the screen, she realized she wasn't
quite ready yet to allow a stranger inside, especially a male
stranger.

"Yes, I did. It's nice to meet you, Alex. Let's walk around
back and I'll show you what I have in mind," she said. She
frowned as she realized there was no car in her driveway.
"Did you walk here?" she asked.

His eyes were a warm blue that stood out against his
tanned face and was complemented by his slightly shaggy
dark hair. "I live three doors up." He pointed up the street to
the Walker home that had been on the market for a while.

"How long have you lived there?"

"I moved in about six weeks ago," he replied as they

walked around the side of the house.

That explained why she didn't know the Walkers had moved out and Mr. Hard Body had moved in. Six weeks ago she'd still been living at her brother Benjamin's house trying to heal from the trauma she'd lived through.

As they reached the backyard she motioned toward the broken brick patio just outside the back door. "What I'd like is a wooden deck big enough to hold a barbecue pit and an umbrella table and, of course, lots of people."

He nodded and pulled a tape measure from his tool belt. "An outdoor entertainment area," he said.

"Exactly," she replied and watched as he began to walk the site. The last thing Brittany had wanted to think about over the past eight months of her life was men. But looking at Alex Crawford definitely gave her a slight flutter of pure feminine pleasure.

Will Brittany be able to heal in the arms of Alex, her hotter-than-sin handyman…or will a second psychopath silence her forever? Find out in
TOOL BELT DEFENDER
Available January 2012
from Harlequin® Romantic Suspense
wherever books are sold.

USA TODAY bestselling author

Penny Jordan

brings you her newest romance

PASSION
AND THE PRINCE

Prince Marco di Lucchesi can't hide his proud
disdain for fiery English rose Lily Wrightington—
or his attraction to her! While touring the palazzos
of northern Italy, the atmosphere heats up...until
shadows from Lily's past come out....

*Can Marco keep his passion under wraps
enough to protect her, or will it unleash itself, too?*

Find out in January 2012!

SPECIAL EDITION

Life, Love and Family

Karen Templeton

introduces

The FORTUNES *of* TEXAS: Whirlwind Romance

When a tornado destroys Red Rock, Texas, Christina Hastings finds herself trapped in the rubble with telecommunications heir Scott Fortune. He's handsome, smart and everything Christina has learned to guard herself against. As they await rescue, an unlikely attraction forms between the two and Scott soon finds himself wanting to know about this mysterious beauty. But can he catch Christina before she runs away from her true feelings?

FORTUNE'S CINDERELLA

Available December 27th wherever books are sold!